THE GRAPHIC NOVEL
Emily Brontë

ORIGINAL TEXT VERSION

Script Adaptation: Seán Michael Wilson
Artwork: John M. Burns
Lettering: Jim Campbell
Design & Layout: Carl Andrews

Associate Editor: Joe Sutliff Sanders
Editor in Chief: Clive Bryant

Wuthering Heights: The Graphic Novel
Original Text Version

Emily Brontë

First US edition published: 2011
Library bound edition published: 2011

Published by: Classical Comics Ltd

Acknowledgments: Every effort has been made to trace copyright holders of
material reproduced in this book. Any rights not acknowledged here will be
acknowledged in subsequent editions if notice is given to Classical Comics Ltd.

All enquiries should be addressed to:
Classical Comics Ltd.
PO Box 7280
Litchborough
Towcester
NN12 9AR
United Kingdom

info@classicalcomics.com
www.classicalcomics.com

Paperback ISBN: 978-1-907127-11-3
Library bound ISBN: 978-1-907127-80-9

Printed in the USA

This book is printed by CG Book Printers using environmentally safe inks, on paper from
responsible sources. This material can be disposed of by recycling, incineration for energy
recovery, composting and biodegradation.

The rights of Seán Michael Wilson, Joe Sutliff Sanders, John M. Burns and Jim Campbell
to be identified as the artists of this work have been asserted in accordance with
the Copyright, Designs and Patents Act 1988 sections 77 and 78.

Contents

Wuthering Heights

Dramatis Personae

Heathcliff

Catherine Earnshaw / Linton
Wife to Edgar Linton

Young Heathcliff

Young Catherine Earnshaw

Mr. Earnshaw
Father to Catherine and Hindley,
also stepfather to Heathcliff

Young Hindley Earnshaw
Catherine's older brother

Adult Hindley Earnshaw

Frances Earnshaw
Hindley's wife

Young Hareton Earnshaw
Son to Hindley and Frances

Older Hareton Earnshaw

Joseph
Servant at Wuthering Heights

Young Edgar Linton
Brother of Isabella Linton

Adult Edgar Linton
Husband to Catherine Earnshaw

Young Isabella Linton
Sister of Edgar Linton

Adult Isabella Linton / Heathcliff
Wife to Heathcliff

Young Cathy Linton
*Daughter to Edgar
and Catherine Linton*

Adult Cathy Linton / Heathcliff
Wife to Linton Heathcliff

Young Linton Heathcliff
*Son to Heathcliff and
Isabella Heathcliff*

Older Linton Heathcliff
Husband to Cathy Linton

Ellen / Nelly Dean
*Servant at Wuthering Heights and
Thrushcross Grange*

Mr. Lockwood
Tenant at Thrushcross Grange

Dr. Kenneth
The local doctor

Zillah
Servant at Wuthering Heights

Wuthering Heights

A FIRST VISIT TO MY *LANDLORD* – THE *SOLITARY* NEIGHBOUR THAT I SHALL BE TROUBLED WITH.

MR. HEATHCLIFF AND I ARE SUCH A *SUITABLE* PAIR TO DIVIDE THE DESOLATION BETWEEN US.

HE LITTLE IMAGINED HOW MY HEART *WARMED* TOWARDS HIM WHEN I BEHELD HIS BLACK EYES WITHDRAW SO *SUSPICIOUSLY* UNDER THEIR BROWS, AS I RODE UP.

MR. HEATHCLIFF?

A *NOD* WAS THE ANSWER.

MR. LOCKWOOD, YOUR NEW *TENANT*, SIR. I DO MYSELF THE HONOUR OF CALLING AS SOON AS *POSSIBLE* AFTER MY ARRIVAL, TO EXPRESS THE HOPE THAT I HAVE NOT *INCONVENIENCED* YOU BY MY *PERSEVERANCE* IN SOLICITING THE OCCUPATION OF THRUSHCROSS GRANGE:

I HEARD *YESTERDAY* YOU HAD HAD SOME THOUGHTS –

THRUSHCROSS GRANGE IS MY *OWN*, SIR. I SHOULD NOT ALLOW *ANY ONE* TO INCONVENIENCE ME, IF I COULD HINDER IT –

WALK IN!

THE "WALK IN" EXPRESSED THE SENTIMENT, "GO TO THE DEUCE": EVEN THE *GATE* MANIFESTED NO SYMPATHISING MOVEMENT TO THE *WORDS*; AND I THINK THAT *CIRCUMSTANCE* DETERMINED ME TO *ACCEPT* THE INVITATION.

JOSEPH, TAKE MR. LOCKWOOD'S **HORSE**; AND BRING UP SOME **WINE**.

The Lord help us!

WUTHERING HEIGHTS IS THE NAME OF MR. HEATHCLIFF'S **DWELLING**. "WUTHERING" BEING A SIGNIFICANT PROVINCIAL ADJECTIVE, DESCRIPTIVE OF THE ATMOSPHERIC **TUMULT** TO WHICH ITS STATION IS **EXPOSED** IN STORMY WEATHER. PURE, BRACING VENTILATION THEY MUST HAVE UP THERE AT ALL TIMES.

1500 HARETON EARNSHAW

BEFORE PASSING THE THRESHOLD, I PAUSED TO ADMIRE A GROTESQUE **CARVING** LAVISHED OVER THE PRINCIPAL DOOR. I DETECTED THE DATE **"1500"** AND THE NAME **"HARETON EARNSHAW"**.

clank-chink p-tank

ONE STEP BROUGHT US INTO THE FAMILY SITTING-ROOM, WITHOUT ANY INTRODUCTORY LOBBY OR PASSAGE: THEY CALL IT HERE *"THE HOUSE"* PRE-EMINENTLY.

IT INCLUDES A KITCHEN AND PARLOUR, GENERALLY; BUT I BELIEVE AT WUTHERING HEIGHTS THE KITCHEN IS FORCED TO RETREAT ALTOGETHER INTO ANOTHER *QUARTER:* AT LEAST I DISTINGUISHED A *CHATTER* OF TONGUES, AND A *CLATTER* OF CULINARY UTENSILS, DEEP WITHIN.

MR. HEATHCLIFF FORMS A *CONTRAST* TO HIS ABODE AND STYLE OF LIVING. HE IS A DARK-SKINNED *GIPSY* IN *ASPECT,* IN DRESS AND MANNERS A *GENTLEMAN:*

THAT IS, AS *MUCH* A GENTLEMAN AS *MANY* A COUNTRY *SQUIRE:* RATHER *SLOVENLY,* PERHAPS, YET NOT LOOKING *AMISS* WITH HIS NEGLIGENCE, BECAUSE HE HAS AN ERECT AND *HANDSOME* FIGURE; AND RATHER *MOROSE.*

POSSIBLY, *SOME* PEOPLE MIGHT SUSPECT HIM OF A DEGREE OF UNDER-BRED *PRIDE;* I HAVE A SYMPATHETIC CHORD WITHIN THAT TELLS ME IT IS *NOTHING* OF THE *SORT:* I KNOW, BY *INSTINCT,* HIS RESERVE SPRINGS FROM AN *AVERSION* TO SHOWY DISPLAYS OF *FEELING* – TO MANIFESTATIONS OF MUTUAL *KINDNESS.* HE'LL LOVE AND HATE *EQUALLY* UNDER COVER, AND ESTEEM IT A SPECIES OF *IMPERTINENCE* TO BE LOVED OR HATED AGAIN.

NO, I'M RUNNING ON TOO *FAST:* I BESTOW MY *OWN* ATTRIBUTES OVER-LIBERALLY ON *HIM.*

MR. HEATHCLIFF MAY HAVE *ENTIRELY* DISSIMILAR REASONS FOR KEEPING HIS *HAND* OUT OF THE *WAY* WHEN HE MEETS A WOULD-BE *ACQUAINTANCE,* TO THOSE WHICH ACTUATE ME.

YOU'D BETTER LET THE DOG **ALONE.** SHE'S NOT ACCUSTOMED TO BE SPOILED —

NOT KEPT FOR A PET.

Grrrrr

STRIDING TO A SIDE DOOR, HE SHOUTED:

JOSEPH!

JOSEPH GAVE **NO** INTIMATION OF ASCENDING; SO HIS MASTER DIVED DOWN TO HIM, LEAVING ME VIS-À-VIS WITH THE **DOGS.**

GRRRAAAH

ARRRGH!

I UNFORTUNATELY INDULGED IN **WINKING** AND MAKING **FACES** AT THE TRIO...

HELP! PLEASE!

GRRRR

WHAT THE **DEVIL** IS THE MATTER?

11

HAPPILY, AN INHABITANT OF THE KITCHEN MADE **MORE** DESPATCH.

grOWf rowf

SHOE, NOW!

WHAT THE DEVIL, INDEED!

THE **HERD** OF POSSESSED **SWINE** COULD HAVE HAD NO WORSE SPIRITS IN THEM THAN THOSE **ANIMALS** OF **YOURS**, SIR.

YOU MIGHT AS WELL LEAVE A STRANGER WITH A BROOD OF **TIGERS**!

THEY WON'T MEDDLE WITH PERSONS WHO TOUCH **NOTHING**. THE DOGS DO **RIGHT** TO BE VIGILANT. TAKE A GLASS OF **WINE?**

NO, THANK YOU.

COME, **COME**, YOU ARE **FLURRIED**, MR. LOCKWOOD. HERE, **TAKE** A LITTLE WINE.

GUESTS ARE SO EXCEEDINGLY **RARE** IN THIS HOUSE THAT I AND MY DOGS, I AM WILLING TO OWN, HARDLY KNOW HOW TO **RECEIVE** THEM.

YOUR **HEALTH**, SIR!

I BOWED AND **RETURNED** THE PLEDGE; BEGINNING TO PERCEIVE THAT IT WOULD BE **FOOLISH** TO SIT SULKING FOR THE MISBEHAVIOUR OF A PACK OF CURS: BESIDES, I FELT **LOATH** TO YIELD THE FELLOW **FURTHER** AMUSEMENT AT **MY** EXPENSE; SINCE HIS HUMOUR TOOK **THAT** TURN.

HE – PROBABLY SWAYED BY PRUDENTIAL CONSIDERATION OF THE **FOLLY** OF OFFENDING A GOOD TENANT – **RELAXED** A LITTLE, AND INTRODUCED WHAT HE SUPPOSED WOULD BE A SUBJECT OF **INTEREST** TO ME, – A DISCOURSE ON THE ADVANTAGES AND DISADVANTAGES OF MY PRESENT PLACE OF **RETIREMENT**.

I FOUND HIM VERY **INTELLIGENT** ON THE TOPICS WE TOUCHED; AND BEFORE I WENT HOME, I WAS ENCOURAGED SO FAR AS TO VOLUNTEER **ANOTHER** VISIT TO-MORROW. HE EVIDENTLY WISHED NO **REPETITION** OF MY INTRUSION. I SHALL GO, NOTWITHSTANDING. IT IS ASTONISHING HOW **SOCIABLE** I FEEL MYSELF COMPARED WITH **HIM**.

CHAPTER II

YESTERDAY AFTERNOON SET IN MISTY AND *COLD*. I HAD A MIND TO SPEND IT BY MY STUDY FIRE, INSTEAD OF WADING THROUGH HEATH AND *MUD* TO WUTHERING HEIGHTS.

ON COMING UP FROM DINNER, HOWEVER, I SAW A SERVANT-GIRL ON HER KNEES SURROUNDED BY BRUSHES AND COAL-SCUTTLES, AND RAISING AN INFERNAL *DUST* AS SHE EXTINGUISHED THE FLAMES WITH HEAPS OF CINDERS.

THIS SPECTACLE DROVE ME *BACK* IMMEDIATELY; I TOOK MY HAT, AND, AFTER A *FOUR-MILES'* WALK, ARRIVED AT HEATHCLIFF'S GARDEN-GATE JUST IN TIME TO ESCAPE THE FIRST FEATHERY FLAKES OF A *SNOW-SHOWER*.

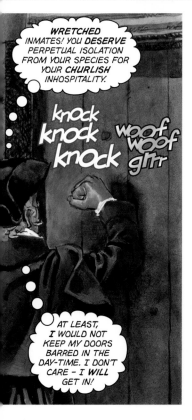

WRETCHED INMATES! YOU *DESERVE* PERPETUAL ISOLATION FROM YOUR SPECIES FOR YOUR *CHURLISH* INHOSPITALITY.

knock knock knock

woof woof grrr

AT LEAST, I WOULD NOT KEEP MY DOORS BARRED IN THE DAY-TIME. I DON'T CARE – I *WILL* GET IN!

WHET ARE YE FOR? – T' *MAISTER'S* DAHN I' T' FOWLD. GOA RAHND BY TH' END UT' LAITH, IF YAH WENT TUH *SPAKE* TULL HIM.

IS THERE *NOBODY* INSIDE TO OPEN THE *DOOR?*

THEY'S *NOBBUT* T' *MISSIS;* AND SHOO'LL *NUT* OPPEN 'T AN YE MAK YER FLAYSOME DINS TILL *NEEGHT.*

WHY? CANNOT *YOU* TELL HER WHO I AM, EH, JOSEPH?

NOR-NE ME! AW'LL HAE *NOA* HEND WI'T.

FOLLOW ME.

13

SIT DOWN. HE'LL BE IN SOON.

ROUGH WEATHER!

I'M AFRAID, MRS. HEATHCLIFF, THE DOOR MUST BEAR THE CONSEQUENCE OF YOUR SERVANTS' LEISURE ATTENDANCE:

I HAD HARD WORK TO MAKE THEM HEAR ME!

YOU SHOULD NOT HAVE COME OUT.

THE SENTIMENT SHE EVINCED HOVERED BETWEEN SCORN AND A KIND OF DESPERATION.

FIVE MINUTES AFTERWARDS, THE ENTRANCE OF MR. HEATHCLIFF RELIEVED ME, IN SOME MEASURE, OF MY UNCOMFORTABLE STATE.

YOU SEE, SIR, I AM COME, ACCORDING TO PROMISE!

AND I FEAR I SHALL BE WEATHER-BOUND FOR HALF AN HOUR, IF YOU CAN AFFORD ME SHELTER DURING THAT SPACE.

HALF AN HOUR? I WONDER YOU SHOULD SELECT THE THICK OF A SNOW-STORM TO RAMBLE ABOUT IN.

DO YOU KNOW THAT YOU RUN A RISK OF BEING LOST IN THE MARSHES?

PEOPLE FAMILIAR WITH THESE MOORS OFTEN MISS THEIR ROAD ON SUCH EVENINGS; AND I CAN TELL YOU THERE IS NO CHANCE OF A CHANGE AT PRESENT.

PERHAPS I CAN GET A GUIDE AMONG YOUR LADS, AND HE MIGHT STAY AT THE GRANGE TILL MORNING – COULD YOU SPARE ME ONE?

NO, I COULD NOT.

OH, INDEED! WELL, THEN, I MUST TRUST TO MY OWN SAGACITY.

IT IS STRANGE HOW CUSTOM CAN MOULD OUR TASTES AND IDEAS: MANY COULD NOT IMAGINE THE EXISTENCE OF HAPPINESS IN A LIFE OF SUCH COMPLETE EXILE FROM THE WORLD AS YOU SPEND, MR. HEATHCLIFF;

YET, I'LL VENTURE TO SAY, THAT, SURROUNDED BY YOUR FAMILY, AND WITH YOUR AMIABLE LADY AS THE PRESIDING GENIUS OVER YOUR HOME AND HEART–

MY AMIABLE LADY! WHERE IS SHE – MY AMIABLE LADY?

MRS. HEATHCLIFF, YOUR WIFE, I MEAN.

WELL, YES – OH! YOU WOULD **INTIMATE** THAT HER **SPIRIT** HAS TAKEN THE POST OF MINISTERING ANGEL, AND GUARDS THE **FORTUNES** OF WUTHERING HEIGHTS, EVEN WHEN HER **BODY** IS GONE. IS **THAT** IT?

I – ERR...

MRS. HEATHCLIFF IS MY DAUGHTER-IN-LAW.

AH, CERTAINLY – I **SEE** NOW: YOU ARE THE **FAVOURED** POSSESSOR OF THE BENEFICENT FAIRY.

UNHAPPY IN YOUR CONJECTURES, SIR! WE **NEITHER** OF US HAVE THE PRIVILEGE OF OWNING YOUR GOOD FAIRY; HER MATE IS **DEAD.**

I SAID SHE WAS MY DAUGHTER-IN-LAW, THEREFORE, SHE MUST HAVE MARRIED MY **SON.**

AND THIS YOUNG MAN IS –

NOT MY SON, ASSUREDLY!

MY **NAME** IS HARETON EARNSHAW, AND I'D COUNSEL YOU TO **RESPECT** IT!

MRS. HEATHCLIFF, YOU MUST **EXCUSE** ME FOR TROUBLING YOU. DO POINT OUT SOME **LANDMARKS** BY WHICH I MAY KNOW MY WAY **HOME.**

TAKE THE ROAD YOU **CAME.** IT IS **BRIEF** ADVICE, BUT AS **SOUND** AS I CAN GIVE.

THEN IF YOU HEAR OF ME BEING DISCOVERED **DEAD** IN A **BOG** OR A **PIT,** YOUR CONSCIENCE WON'T WHISPER THAT IT IS PARTLY **YOUR** FAULT?

I CANNOT ESCORT YOU. THEY WOULDN'T LET **ME** GO TO THE END OF THE GARDEN **WALL.**

ARE THERE **NO** BOYS AT THE FARM?

NO.

THEN, IT FOLLOWS THAT I AM COMPELLED TO **STAY.** I CAN SLEEP ON A **CHAIR** IN THIS ROOM.

NO, **NO!** A STRANGER IS A **STRANGER,** BE HE RICH OR POOR: IT WILL NOT SUIT ME TO PERMIT **ANY ONE** THE RANGE OF THE PLACE WHILE I AM OFF **GUARD!**

WITH THIS INSULT, MY *PATIENCE* WAS AT AN *END*.

I *PUSHED* MY WAY OUT.

MAISTER, MAISTER, HE'S *STALING* T' LANTHERN!

I WILL SEND IT *BACK* ON THE MORROW!

HEY, GNASHER! HEY, DOG! HEY WOLF, HOLLD HIM, HOLLD HIM!

HARGH!

I WAS FORCED TO *LIE* TILL THEIR MALIGNANT MASTERS *PLEASED* TO *DELIVER* ME. TREMBLING WITH *WRATH*, I ORDERED THE MISCREANTS TO LET ME OUT – ON THEIR PERIL TO KEEP ME ONE MINUTE LONGER – WITH SEVERAL INCOHERENT THREATS OF *RETALIATION* THAT, IN THEIR INDEFINITE DEPTH OF VIRULENCY, SMACKED OF *KING LEAR*.

grraargh

I DON'T KNOW *WHAT* WOULD HAVE CONCLUDED THE SCENE, HAD IT NOT BEEN FOR *ZILLAH*, THE STOUT HOUSEWIFE.

grrrr

Ohhh...

WELL, I WONDER WHAT YOU'LL HAVE AGAIT *NEXT*! ARE WE GOING TO *MURDER* FOLK ON OUR VERY *DOOR-STONES*?

I SEE THIS HOUSE WILL *NEVER* DO FOR ME – LOOK AT T' POOR LAD, HE'S FAIR *CHOKING*!

WISHT, WISHT; YOU MUN'N'T GO ON SO. THERE NOW, HOLD YE STILL.

SHE PULLED ME INTO THE *KITCHEN* AND SPLASHED A PINT OF *ICY WATER* DOWN MY NECK. I WAS *SICK* EXCEEDINGLY, AND DIZZY AND FAINT;

AND THUS COMPELLED, PERFORCE, TO *ACCEPT* LODGINGS UNDER *HIS* ROOF. HE TOLD ZILLAH TO GIVE ME A GLASS OF *BRANDY*. SHE OBEYED HIS ORDERS AND USHERED ME TO *BED*.

CHAPTER III

WHILE LEADING THE WAY UPSTAIRS, SHE RECOMMENDED THAT I SHOULD *HIDE* THE CANDLE, AND NOT MAKE A *NOISE*; FOR HER *MASTER* HAD AN ODD NOTION ABOUT THE *CHAMBER* SHE WOULD PUT ME IN, AND NEVER LET *ANYBODY* LODGE THERE *WILLINGLY*.

WHAT *IS* THE REASON?

I DON'T *KNOW*. I HAVE ONLY LIVED HERE A *YEAR* OR TWO; AND THERE ARE SO MANY QUEER GOINGS ON, I CAN'T *BEGIN* TO BE CURIOUS.

TOO *STUPEFIED* TO BE CURIOUS MYSELF, I FASTENED MY DOOR AND GLANCED ROUND FOR THE BED.

IT WAS A SINGULAR SORT OF *OLD-FASHIONED* COUCH, AND THE *LEDGE* OF A *WINDOW* SERVED AS A TABLE.

THE LEDGE HAD A FEW MILDEWED *BOOKS* PILED UP IN ONE CORNER; AND IT WAS COVERED WITH *WRITING* SCRATCHED ON THE PAINT, THAT WAS NOTHING BUT A NAME REPEATED IN ALL KINDS OF CHARACTERS – *CATHERINE EARNSHAW*, VARIED TO CATHERINE *HEATHCLIFF*, AND AGAIN TO CATHERINE *LINTON*.

I TOOK UP EACH BOOK UNTIL I HAD EXAMINED ALL. CATHERINE'S LIBRARY WAS *SELECT*, AND ITS STATE PROVED IT TO HAVE BEEN *WELL USED*.

BIBLE

Catherine Earnshaw
HER BOOK

IN VAPID LISTLESSNESS, MY EYES *CLOSED*;

BUT THEY HAD NOT RESTED FIVE MINUTES WHEN A GLARE OF *LETTERS* STARTED FROM THE DARK, AS VIVID AS *SPECTRES.* THE AIR *SWARMED* WITH CATHERINES...

...AND I *ROUSED* MYSELF TO DISPEL THE OBTRUSIVE NAME.

VERY ILL AT EASE UNDER THE INFLUENCE OF *COLD* AND *NAUSEA,* I SAT UP AND SPREAD OPEN A MUSTY TESTAMENT.

SCARCELY *ONE* CHAPTER HAD ESCAPED PEN-AND-INK COMMENTARY COVERING EVERY *MORSEL* OF BLANK THAT THE PRINTER HAD LEFT. *SOME* WERE DETACHED SENTENCES; OTHER PARTS TOOK THE FORM OF A REGULAR *DIARY.*

AN *IMMEDIATE* INTEREST KINDLED WITHIN ME FOR THE UNKNOWN CATHERINE...

An awful Sunday!
I wish my father were back again.
Hindley is a detestable substitute —
his conduct to Heathcliff is atrocious —
H. and I are going to rebel —
we took our initiatory step this evening.

All day had been flooding with rain; we could not go to church, so Joseph must needs get up a congregation in the garret; and, while Hindley and his wife basked downstairs before a comfortable fire — doing anything but reading their Bibles, I'll answer for it — Heathcliff, myself, and the unhappy ploughboy were commanded to take our prayer-books.

The service lasted precisely three hours.

T' MAISTER NOBBUT JUST **BURIED,** AND SABBATH NUT OE'RED, UND T' SAHND UH'T GOSPEL STILL I' YER LUGS, AND YAH **DARR** BE LAIKING!

SHAME ON YE! SIT YE DAHN, ILL CHILDER! THEY'S GOOD BOOKS ENEUGH IF YE'LL **READ** 'EM: SIT YE DAHN, AND THINK UH YER **SOWLS!**

FLING!

MAISTER HINDLEY! MAISTER, COOM **HITHER!** MISS CATHY'S **RIVEN** TH' BACK OFF "TH' HELMET O' SALVATION," UN' HEATHCLIFF'S **PAWSED** HIS FIT INTUH T' FIRST PART UH "T' BROOAD WAY TO DESTRUCTION!"

IT'S FAIR **FLAYSOME** UT YAH LET 'EM GOA ON THIS GAIT. ECH! TH' OWD MAN UD UH LACED 'EM **PROPERLY** — BUD HE'S GOAN!

Hindley hurried up from his paradise on the hearth and hurled us both into the back-kitchen.

How little did I dream that Hindley would ever make me cry so! My head aches, till I cannot keep it on the pillow; and still I can't give over.

Poor Heathcliff! Hindley calls him a vagabond, and won't let him sit with us, nor eat with us any more; and, he says, he and I must not play together, and threatens to turn him out of the house if we break his orders.

He has been blaming our father (how dared he?) for treating H. too liberally; and swears he will reduce him to his right place —

I BEGAN TO NOD **DROWSILY** OVER THE DIM PAGE...

THE **BRANCH** OF A FIR-TREE TOUCHED MY LATTICE AS THE BLAST OF GUSTY WIND **WAILED** BY, AND **RATTLED** ITS DRY CONES AGAINST THE PANES.

tap tap tap

IT **ANNOYED** ME SO MUCH, THAT I RESOLVED TO **SILENCE** IT, IF POSSIBLE.

tap tap tap

BUT THE HOOK WAS **SOLDERED** INTO THE STAPLE.

I **must** stop it, nonetheless.

I STRETCHED AN ARM OUT TO **SEIZE** THE IMPORTUNATE **BRANCH**...

SMAS

...INSTEAD OF WHICH, MY FINGERS **CLOSED** ON THE **FINGERS** OF A LITTLE, ICE-COLD **HAND!**

LET ME IN – **LET ME IN!**

WHO **ARE** YOU?

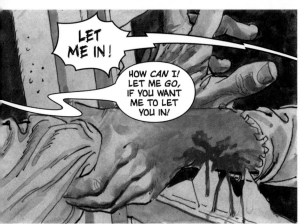

I'M SORRY I DISTURBED YOU.

OH, GOD CONFOUND YOU, MR. LOCKWOOD! WHO SHOWED YOU UP TO THIS ROOM?

IT WAS YOUR SERVANT, ZILLAH. I SUPPOSE SHE WANTED TO GET PROOF THE PLACE WAS HAUNTED.

WELL, IT IS --

WHAT DO YOU MEAN?

IF THE LITTLE FIEND HAD GOT IN AT THE WINDOW, SHE PROBABLY WOULD HAVE STRANGLED ME!

THAT MINX, CATHERINE LINTON, OR EARNSHAW, OR HOWEVER SHE WAS CALLED – WICKED LITTLE SOUL!

SHE TOLD ME SHE HAD BEEN WALKING THE EARTH THESE TWENTY YEARS: A JUST PUNISHMENT FOR HER MORTAL TRANSGRESSIONS, I'VE NO DOUBT!

WHAT CAN YOU MEAN BY TALKING IN THIS WAY TO ME! HOW DARE YOU, UNDER MY ROOF?

GOD, HE'S MAD TO SPEAK SO!

SHOULD I RESENT THIS LANGUAGE OR PURSUE AN EXPLANATION?

TAKE THE CANDLE, AND GO WHERE YOU PLEASE. KEEP OUT OF THE YARD, THOUGH, THE DOGS ARE UNCHAINED.

BUT, AWAY WITH YOU!

COME IN! COME IN! CATHY, DO COME.

OH, DO – ONCE MORE! OH! MY HEART'S DARLING! HEAR ME THIS TIME, CATHERINE, AT LAST!

THE SPECTRE SHOWED NO SIGN OF BEING.

I DECLINED BREAKFAST AND, AT THE FIRST GLIMPSE OF DAWN, TOOK AN OPPORTUNITY OF *ESCAPING* INTO THE FREE AIR.

THE DISTANCE FROM THE GATE TO THE GRANGE IS *TWO MILES;* I BELIEVE I MANAGED TO MAKE IT FOUR, WHAT WITH LOSING MYSELF AMONG THE TREES, AND SINKING UP TO THE *NECK* IN SNOW: A PREDICAMENT WHICH ONLY THOSE WHO HAVE EXPERIENCED IT CAN *APPRECIATE.*

AT ANY RATE, WHATEVER WERE MY WANDERINGS, THE CLOCK CHIMED *TWELVE* AS I ENTERED THE HOUSE; AND THAT GAVE EXACTLY AN *HOUR* FOR EVERY *MILE* OF THE USUAL WAY FROM WUTHERING HEIGHTS.

CHAPTER IV

YOU HAVE LIVED HERE A *CONSIDERABLE* TIME. DID YOU NOT SAY *SIXTEEN* YEARS?

EIGHTEEN, SIR: I CAME WHEN THE *MISTRESS* WAS MARRIED, TO WAIT ON HER; AFTER SHE DIED, THE MASTER RETAINED ME FOR HIS HOUSEKEEPER.

AH, TIMES ARE *GREATLY* CHANGED SINCE THEN!

UNDER *PRETENCE* OF GAINING INFORMATION CONCERNING THE NECESSITIES OF MY ESTABLISHMENT, I DESIRED MRS. DEAN TO SIT DOWN.

WHY DOES MR. HEATHCLIFF *LET* THRUSHCROSS GRANGE AND PREFER TO LIVE IN A SITUATION AND RESIDENCE SO MUCH *INFERIOR?*

IS HE NOT *RICH* ENOUGH TO KEEP THE ESTATE IN GOOD *ORDER?*

RICH SIR! HE HAS, NOBODY *KNOWS* WHAT MONEY, AND EVERY YEAR IT *INCREASES.*

AS SOON AS HE HEARD OF A GOOD TENANT HE COULD NOT HAVE *BORNE* TO MISS THE CHANCE OF GETTING A FEW HUNDREDS *MORE.*

HE HAD A *SON* IT SEEMS?

YES, HE *HAD* ONE – HE IS *DEAD.*

AND THAT YOUNG LADY, MRS. HEATHCLIFF IS HIS *WIDOW?*

YES – SHE IS MY LATE MASTER'S *DAUGHTER:* CATHERINE LINTON WAS HER *MAIDEN* NAME. I *NURSED* HER, POOR THING!

AND *WHO* IS THAT HARETON EARNSHAW?

HE IS THE *LATE* MRS. LINTON'S *NEPHEW.*

THE YOUNG LADY'S *COUSIN,* THEN?

YES; AND HER *HUSBAND* WAS HER *COUSIN* ALSO:

ONE ON THE *MOTHER'S,* THE OTHER ON THE *FATHER'S* SIDE:

HEATHCLIFF MARRIED MR. LINTON'S *SISTER.*

WELL, MRS. DEAN, IT WILL BE A **CHARITABLE** DEED TO TELL ME SOMETHING OF MY NEIGHBOURS: I FEEL I SHALL NOT **REST**, IF I GO TO BED; SO BE GOOD ENOUGH TO SIT AND **CHAT** AN HOUR.

OH, **CERTAINLY**, SIR! I'LL JUST FETCH A LITTLE **SEWING**, AND THEN I'LL SIT AS LONG AS YOU **PLEASE**.

BEFORE I CAME TO LIVE **HERE**, I WAS ALMOST **ALWAYS** AT WUTHERING HEIGHTS; BECAUSE MY **MOTHER** HAD NURSED MR. **HINDLEY** EARNSHAW, THAT WAS HARETON'S **FATHER**, AND I GOT USED TO **PLAYING** WITH THE CHILDREN:

I RAN **ERRANDS** TOO, AND HELPED TO MAKE **HAY**, AND HUNG ABOUT THE FARM READY FOR **ANYTHING** THAT ANYBODY WOULD **SET** ME TO.

ONE FINE SUMMER MORNING, MR. EARNSHAW, THE **OLD** MASTER, WENT OFF TO LIVERPOOL, **WALKING** THE SIXTY MILES EACH WAY. HE KISSED HIS CHILDREN **GOODBYE**, AND SET OFF. IT SEEMED A LONG WHILE TO US ALL – THE THREE DAYS OF HIS ABSENCE – AND OFTEN DID LITTLE CATHY ASK WHEN HE WOULD BE **HOME**.

JUST ABOUT ELEVEN O'CLOCK, THE DOOR LATCH WAS RAISED, AND IN STEPPED THE **MASTER**.

SEE **HERE**, WIFE! I WAS NEVER SO **BEATEN** WITH ANYTHING IN MY LIFE: BUT YOU MUST E'EN TAKE IT AS A GIFT OF **GOD**; THOUGH IT'S AS **DARK** ALMOST AS IF IT CAME FROM THE DEVIL.

THIS WAS **HEATHCLIFF'S** FIRST INTRODUCTION TO THE FAMILY. THEY CHRISTENED HIM "HEATHCLIFF" AS IT WAS THE NAME OF A **SON** WHO **DIED** IN CHILDHOOD, AND IT HAS SERVED HIM EVER **SINCE**, BOTH FOR **CHRISTIAN** AND **SURNAME**.

MISS CATHY AND HE BECAME **VERY** THICK; BUT HINDLEY **HATED** HIM: AND TO SAY THE TRUTH **I** DID THE **SAME**; AND WE **PLAGUED** AND WENT **ON** WITH HIM **SHAMEFULLY.**

HE SEEMED A **SULLEN,** PATIENT CHILD; **HARDENED,** PERHAPS TO ILL-TREATMENT: HE WOULD **STAND** HINDLEY'S **BLOWS** WITHOUT WINKING OR SHEDDING A **TEAR.**

OLD **EARNSHAW** WAS **FURIOUS** WHEN HE DISCOVERED HIS **SON** PERSECUTING THE POOR, FATHERLESS **CHILD,** AS HE CALLED HIM.

HE **TOOK** TO HEATHCLIFF STRANGELY, BELIEVING **ALL** HE SAID, AND PETTING HIM UP **FAR** ABOVE CATHY, WHO WAS TOO MISCHIEVOUS AND **WAYWARD** FOR A **FAVOURITE.**

SO, FROM THE VERY **BEGINNING,** HE BRED **BAD** FEELING IN THE HOUSE.

AT MRS. EARNSHAW'S **DEATH,** WHICH HAPPENED IN LESS THAN **TWO YEARS** AFTER, THE YOUNG MASTER HAD LEARNT TO REGARD HIS FATHER AS AN **OPPRESSOR** RATHER THAN A **FRIEND,** AND HEATHCLIFF AS A **USURPER** OF HIS PARENT'S **AFFECTIONS** AND HIS **PRIVILEGES,** AND HE GREW **BITTER.**

I WAS **SURPRISED** TO WITNESS HOW **COOLLY** THE CHILD GATHERED HIMSELF UP. HE COMPLAINED SO **SELDOM** OF SUCH STIRS AS THESE, THAT I **REALLY** THOUGHT HIM **NOT** VINDICTIVE:

I WAS **DECEIVED** COMPLETELY, AS YOU WILL HEAR.

IN THE COURSE OF TIME MR. EARNSHAW BEGAN TO *FAIL.*

HE HAD BEEN ACTIVE AND *HEALTHY,* YET HIS STRENGTH *LEFT* HIM SUDDENLY; AND WHEN HE WAS CONFINED TO THE *CHIMNEY-CORNER* HE GREW GRIEVOUSLY *IRRITABLE.*

CHAPTER V

A *NOTHING* VEXED HIM; AND SUSPECTED *SLIGHTS* OF HIS *AUTHORITY* NEARLY THREW HIM INTO *FITS.*

THIS WAS *ESPECIALLY* TO BE REMARKED IF ANY ONE ATTEMPTED TO *IMPOSE* UPON, OR *DOMINEER* OVER, HIS FAVOURITE, *HEATHCLIFF.*

AT LAST, OUR CURATE ADVISED THAT HINDLEY SHOULD BE SENT TO *COLLEGE;* AND MR. EARNSHAW AGREED, THOUGH WITH A *HEAVY* SPIRIT, FOR HE SAID – "HINDLEY WAS *NOUGHT,* AND WOULD *NEVER* THRIVE AS WHERE HE WANDERED."

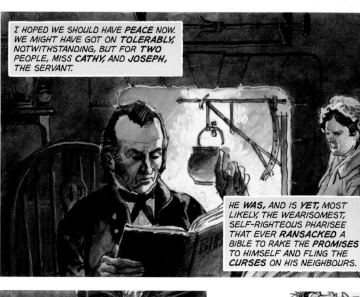

I HOPED WE SHOULD HAVE *PEACE* NOW. WE MIGHT HAVE GOT ON *TOLERABLY,* NOTWITHSTANDING, BUT FOR *TWO* PEOPLE, MISS *CATHY,* AND *JOSEPH,* THE SERVANT.

HE *WAS,* AND IS *YET,* MOST LIKELY, THE WEARISOMEST, SELF-RIGHTEOUS PHARISEE THAT EVER *RANSACKED* A BIBLE TO RAKE THE *PROMISES* TO HIMSELF AND FLING THE *CURSES* ON HIS NEIGHBOURS.

MISS CATHY PUT *ALL* OF US PAST OUR *PATIENCE* FIFTY TIMES AND OFTENER IN A DAY: WE HAD NOT A *MINUTE'S* SECURITY THAT SHE WOULDN'T BE IN *MISCHIEF.*

A WILD, *WICKED* SLIP SHE WAS.

SHE WAS *MUCH* TOO *FOND* OF HEATHCLIFF. THE *GREATEST* PUNISHMENT WE COULD *INVENT* FOR HER WAS TO KEEP HER *SEPARATE* FROM *HIM.*

ONE OCTOBER EVENING, MISS CATHY HAD BEEN *SICK*, AND THAT MADE HER *STILL*.

WHY CANST THOU NOT ALWAYS BE A *GOOD* LASS, CATHY?

WHY CANNOT *YOU* ALWAYS BE A GOOD *MAN*, FATHER?

OH, CATHY!

I'M SORRY DEAR FATHER – LET ME SING YOU TO SLEEP.

La, tra-la. Fa, la la.

AFTER HALF-AN-HOUR, JOSEPH GOT UP AND SAID THAT HE MUST *ROUSE* THE MASTER FOR *PRAYERS* AND *BED*.

FRAME UP-STAIRS NOW, AND MAKE LITTLE DIN. I 'AV SUMMUT TO DO.

I SHALL BID FATHER *GOOD-NIGHT* FIRST.

OH, HE'S DEAD, HEATHCLIFF! *HE'S DEAD!*

AND THEY BOTH SET UP A *HEART-BREAKING* CRY.

27

MR. HINDLEY CAME HOME TO THE FUNERAL; AND – A THING THAT *AMAZED* US, AND SET THE NEIGHBOURS *GOSSIPING* RIGHT AND LEFT – HE BROUGHT A *WIFE* WITH HIM.

CHAPTER VI

WHAT SHE *WAS*, AND WHERE SHE WAS *BORN*, HE NEVER INFORMED US: PROBABLY, SHE HAD NEITHER *MONEY* NOR *NAME* TO RECOMMEND HER, OR HE WOULD SCARCELY HAVE *KEPT* THE UNION FROM HIS *FATHER*.

SHE WAS RATHER *THIN*, BUT *YOUNG*, AND *FRESH* COMPLEXIONED, AND HER EYES *SPARKLED* AS BRIGHT AS DIAMONDS. I DID REMARK, TO BE SURE, THAT MOUNTING THE STAIRS MADE HER *BREATHE* VERY QUICK; THAT THE LEAST SUDDEN *NOISE* SET HER ALL IN A *QUIVER*, AND THAT SHE *COUGHED* TROUBLESOMELY SOMETIMES: BUT I KNEW *NOTHING* OF WHAT THESE SYMPTOMS PORTENDED, AND HAD NO IMPULSE TO *SYMPATHISE* WITH HER.

YOUNG EARNSHAW WAS *ALTERED* CONSIDERABLY IN THE THREE YEARS OF HIS ABSENCE. HE HAD GROWN *SPARER*, AND LOST HIS *COLOUR*, AND SPOKE AND DRESSED QUITE *DIFFERENTLY*; AND, ON THE VERY *DAY* OF HIS RETURN, HE TOLD JOSEPH AND ME WE MUST THENCEFORTH QUARTER OURSELVES IN THE *BACK-KITCHEN*, AND LEAVE THE HOUSE FOR *HIM*.

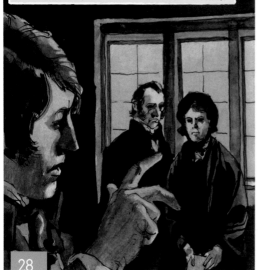

HE DROVE *HEATHCLIFF* FROM THEIR COMPANY TO THE *SERVANTS*, DEPRIVED HIM OF THE INSTRUCTIONS OF THE *CURATE*, AND INSISTED THAT HE SHOULD *LABOUR* OUT OF DOORS INSTEAD; COMPELLING HIM TO DO SO AS *HARD* AS ANY *OTHER* LAD ON THE *FARM*.

ONLY *JOSEPH* AND THE *CURATE* REPRIMANDED HIS CARELESSNESS WHEN THEY *ABSENTED* THEMSELVES; AND THAT *REMINDED* HIM TO ORDER HEATHCLIFF A *FLOGGING*, AND CATHERINE A *FAST* FROM DINNER OR SUPPER.

BUT IT WAS ONE OF THEIR *CHIEF* AMUSEMENTS TO RUN AWAY TO THE *MOORS* IN THE MORNING AND REMAIN THERE ALL *DAY*, AND THE AFTER *PUNISHMENT* GREW A MERE THING TO *LAUGH* AT.

HEATHCLIFF *BORE* HIS DEGRADATION PRETTY *WELL* AT FIRST, BECAUSE CATHY TAUGHT HIM WHAT SHE *LEARNT*, AND WORKED OR PLAYED WITH HIM IN THE *FIELDS*.

THEY BOTH PROMISED FAIR TO GROW UP AS *RUDE* AS *SAVAGES*; THE YOUNG MASTER BEING ENTIRELY *NEGLIGENT* HOW THEY *BEHAVED*, AND WHAT THEY *DID*, SO THEY KEPT *CLEAR* OF HIM.

THE CURATE MIGHT SET AS *MANY* CHAPTERS AS HE PLEASED FOR CATHERINE TO GET BY HEART, AND JOSEPH MIGHT *THRASH* HEATHCLIFF TILL HIS ARM ACHED; THEY FORGOT *EVERYTHING* THE MINUTE THEY WERE *TOGETHER* AGAIN.

ONE SUNDAY EVENING, IT CHANCED THAT THEY WERE *BANISHED* FROM THE SITTING-ROOM, FOR MAKING A NOISE, OR A LIGHT OFFENCE OF THE KIND; AND WHEN I WENT TO *CALL* THEM TO SUPPER, I COULD DISCOVER THEM *NOWHERE*.

HINDLEY IN A *PASSION* TOLD US TO *BOLT* THE *DOORS*, AND SWORE *NOBODY* SHOULD LET THEM *IN* THAT NIGHT.

THE HOUSEHOLD WENT TO BED; AND I, TOO ANXIOUS TO LIE DOWN, *OPENED* MY LATTICE AND PUT MY HEAD OUT TO HEARKEN, THOUGH IT *RAINED*: DETERMINED TO *ADMIT* THEM IN SPITE OF THE PROHIBITION, SHOULD THEY *RETURN*.

29

IN A WHILE, I DISTINGUISHED **STEPS** COMING UP THE ROAD, AND THE LIGHT OF A LANTERN GLIMMERED THROUGH THE GATE. THERE WAS **HEATHCLIFF**, BY HIMSELF: IT GAVE ME A **START** TO SEE HIM **ALONE**.

WHERE IS MISS CATHERINE? NO **ACCIDENT**, I HOPE?

AT **THRUSHCROSS GRANGE** – AND I WOULD HAVE BEEN THERE **TOO**, BUT THEY HAD NOT THE **MANNERS** TO ASK ME TO STAY.

CATHY AND I ESCAPED FROM THE WASH-HOUSE TO HAVE A **RAMBLE** AT **LIBERTY**, AND GETTING A GLIMPSE OF THE GRANGE **LIGHTS**,

WE THOUGHT WE WOULD JUST GO AND SEE WHETHER THE **LINTONS** PASSED **THEIR** SUNDAY EVENINGS STANDING **SHIVERING** IN CORNERS, WHILE **THEIR** FATHER AND MOTHER SAT **EATING** AND DRINKING, AND SINGING AND **LAUGHING**.

WE RAN FROM THE TOP OF THE HEIGHTS TO THE PARK, WITHOUT **STOPPING**. WE CREPT THROUGH A BROKEN **HEDGE** --

-- AND PLANTED OURSELVES ON A **FLOWER-POT** UNDER THE DRAWING-ROOM **WINDOW**.

OLD MR. AND MRS. LINTON WERE NOT **THERE**; EDGAR AND HIS SISTER HAD IT ENTIRELY TO **THEMSELVES**. SHOULDN'T THEY HAVE BEEN **HAPPY**?

WE SHOULD HAVE THOUGHT OURSELVES IN **HEAVEN**! BUT NO, THEY **QUARRELLED**. THE **IDIOTS**!

WE *LAUGHED* OUTRIGHT AT THE PETTED THINGS; WE DID *DESPISE* THEM!

THE LINTONS *HEARD* US, AND SHOT LIKE *ARROWS* TO THE DOOR.

ha ha ha ha ha

OH, PAPA, OH!

OH, MAMMA, MAMMA!

WE FELT WE HAD BETTER *FLEE.*

KEEP *FAST,* SKULKER, KEEP *FAST!*

RUN, HEATHCLIFF, *RUN!*

A *BEAST* OF A SERVANT CAME UP.

WHAT *PREY,* ROBERT?

SKULKER HAS CAUGHT A LITTLE *GIRL,* SIR; AND THERE'S A LAD HERE, WHO LOOKS AN *OUT-AND-OUTER!*

VERY LIKE, THE *ROBBERS* WERE FOR PUTTING THEM THROUGH THE *WINDOW* TO OPEN THE *DOORS* TO THE GANG.

THAT IS MISS **EARNSHAW.** AND LOOK HOW SKULKER HAS **BITTEN** HER – HOW HER FOOT **BLEEDS!**

BUT WHO **IS** THIS? WHERE DID SHE **PICK UP** THIS COMPANION?

*¿#!, THEY ARE ALL *¿#!

OHO! I DECLARE HE IS THAT STRANGE **ACQUISITION** MY LATE **NEIGHBOUR** MADE, IN HIS JOURNEY TO LIVERPOOL – A LITTLE **LASCAR,** OR AN AMERICAN OR SPANISH **CASTAWAY.**

A **WICKED** BOY, AT ALL EVENTS, AND QUITE **UNFIT** FOR A **DECENT** HOUSE.

DID YOU NOTICE HIS **LANGUAGE?** I'M **SHOCKED** THAT MY CHILDREN SHOULD HAVE **HEARD** IT.

I RESUMED MY STATION AS **SPY;** BECAUSE, IF CATHERINE HAD WISHED TO **RETURN,** I INTENDED **SHATTERING** THEIR GREAT GLASS **PANES** TO A MILLION OF **FRAGMENTS,** UNLESS THEY LET HER OUT.

I SAW THEY WERE FULL OF STUPID **ADMIRATION;** SHE IS SO IMMEASURABLY **SUPERIOR** TO THEM – TO **EVERYBODY** ON **EARTH,** IS SHE NOT, **NELLY?**

THERE WILL **MORE** COME OF THIS BUSINESS THAN YOU **RECKON** ON. YOU ARE **INCURABLE,** HEATHCLIFF; AND MR. HINDLEY WILL HAVE TO PROCEED TO **EXTREMITIES,** SEE IF HE WON'T.

CHAPTER VII

CATHY STAYED AT THRUSHCROSS GRANGE *FIVE WEEKS:* TILL *CHRISTMAS.*

BY THAT TIME HER ANKLE WAS *THOROUGHLY* CURED, AND HER MANNERS *MUCH* IMPROVED.

THE MISTRESS VISITED HER *OFTEN* IN THE INTERVAL, AND COMMENCED HER PLAN OF *REFORM* BY TRYING TO *RAISE* HER *SELF-RESPECT* WITH FINE CLOTHES AND *FLATTERY,* WHICH SHE TOOK *READILY.*

SO THAT, INSTEAD OF A WILD, HATLESS LITTLE *SAVAGE* JUMPING INTO THE HOUSE, AND RUSHING TO SQUEEZE US ALL *BREATHLESS,* THERE LIGHTED FROM A HANDSOME BLACK PONY A VERY *DIGNIFIED* PERSON.

HINDLEY LIFTED HER FROM HER HORSE.

WHY, CATHY, YOU ARE QUITE A *BEAUTY!*

I SHOULD SCARCELY HAVE *KNOWN* YOU: YOU LOOK LIKE A LADY NOW. ISABELLA LINTON IS NOT TO BE *COMPARED* WITH HER, IS SHE, FRANCES?

ISABELLA HAS NOT HER *NATURAL* ADVANTAGES, BUT SHE MUST *MIND* AND NOT GROW *WILD* AGAIN HERE.

ELLEN, HELP MISS CATHERINE OFF WITH HER *THINGS.*

STAY, DEAR, YOU WILL DISARRANGE YOUR *CURLS* – LET ME *UNTIE* YOUR HAT.

33

WHERE IS HEATHCLIFF?

HEATHCLIFF, YOU MAY COME FORWARD. YOU MAY COME AND WISH MISS CATHERINE WELCOME, LIKE THE OTHER SERVANTS.

WHY, HOW VERY BLACK AND CROSS YOU LOOK! AND HOW - HOW FUNNY AND GRIM!

BUT THAT'S BECAUSE I'M USED TO EDGAR AND ISABELLA LINTON.

WELL, HEATHCLIFF, HAVE YOU FORGOTTEN ME?

I SHALL NOT STAND TO BE LAUGHED AT.

I SHALL NOT BEAR IT!

I DID NOT MEAN TO LAUGH AT YOU. I COULD NOT HINDER MYSELF. IT WAS ONLY THAT YOU LOOKED ODD. IF YOU WASH YOUR FACE, AND BRUSH YOUR HAIR, IT WILL BE ALL RIGHT: BUT YOU ARE SO DIRTY!

I SHALL BE AS DIRTY AS I PLEASE:

AND I LIKE TO BE DIRTY, AND I WILL BE DIRTY.

I LATER REMEMBERED **OLD EARNSHAW'S FONDNESS** FOR HEATHCLIFF, AND HIS **DREAD** LEST HE SHOULD SUFFER NEGLECT AFTER DEATH HAD **REMOVED** HIM: AND THAT NATURALLY **LED** ME TO CONSIDER THE POOR LAD'S SITUATION **NOW**.

MAKE **HASTE**, HEATHCLIFF. CATHY COMES OUT, AND YOU CAN SIT **TOGETHER**.

HE NEVER TURNED HIS HEAD TOWARDS ME, AND I GOT NO **ANSWER** FROM HIM.

IN THE MORNING HE ROSE **EARLY**; AND, AS IT WAS A HOLIDAY, CARRIED HIS ILL-HUMOUR ONTO THE **MOORS**; NOT RE-APPEARING TILL THE FAMILY WERE DEPARTED FOR **CHURCH**...

...FASTING AND REFLECTION SEEMED TO HAVE BROUGHT HIM TO A **BETTER** SPIRIT. HE HUNG ABOUT ME FOR A WHILE, AND HAVING SCREWED UP HIS COURAGE, EXCLAIMED **ABRUPTLY**:

NELLY, MAKE ME DECENT, I'M GOING TO BE GOOD.

HIGH **TIME**, HEATHCLIFF; YOU HAVE **GRIEVED** CATHERINE: SHE'S SORRY SHE EVER CAME **HOME**, I DARESAY!

SHE **CRIED** WHEN I TOLD HER YOU WERE **OFF** AGAIN THIS MORNING.

WELL, **I** CRIED LAST NIGHT, AND I HAD MORE **REASON** TO CRY THAN SHE.

YES, **YOU** HAD THE REASON OF GOING TO BED WITH A **PROUD** HEART AND AN **EMPTY** STOMACH. BUT I'LL ARRANGE YOU SO THAT EDGAR LINTON SHALL LOOK QUITE A **DOLL** BESIDE YOU. YOU COULD KNOCK HIM **DOWN** IN A **TWINKLING**.

BUT, NELLY, IF I KNOCKED HIM DOWN **TWENTY** TIMES, THAT WOULDN'T MAKE HIM **LESS** HANDSOME AND ME **MORE** SO.

I WISH I DRESSED AND BEHAVED AS WELL, AND HAD A CHANCE OF BEING AS **RICH** AS HE WILL BE!

A GOOD HEART WILL HELP YOU TO A **BONNY** FACE, MY LAD.

NOW THAT WE'VE DONE **WASHING**, AND **COMBING**, AND **SULKING** – TELL ME WHETHER YOU DON'T THINK YOURSELF RATHER **HANDSOME**?

I'LL TELL YOU, I DO.

YOU'RE FIT FOR A **PRINCE** IN DISGUISE.

WHO KNOWS BUT YOUR **FATHER** WAS **EMPEROR** OF CHINA, AND YOUR **MOTHER** AN **INDIAN QUEEN**, EACH OF THEM ABLE TO **BUY UP**, WITH **ONE** WEEK'S INCOME, WUTHERING HEIGHTS AND THRUSHCROSS GRANGE **TOGETHER**? WERE I IN **YOUR** PLACE, I WOULD **FRAME** HIGH NOTIONS OF MY BIRTH --

-- AND THE THOUGHTS OF WHAT I WAS SHOULD GIVE ME **COURAGE** AND DIGNITY TO SUPPORT THE **OPPRESSIONS** OF A LITTLE **FARMER**!

BEGONE, YOU VAGABOND! **WHAT**! YOU ARE ATTEMPTING THE COXCOMB, ARE YOU?

WAIT TILL I GET **HOLD** OF THOSE ELEGANT **LOCKS** - SEE IF I WON'T PULL THEM A BIT **LONGER**!

THEY ARE LONG ENOUGH **ALREADY**, I WONDER THEY DON'T MAKE HIS HEAD **ACHE**. IT'S LIKE A COLT'S **MANE** OVER HIS **EYES**!

HEATHCLIFF WAS NOT PREPARED TO **ENDURE** THE APPEARANCE OF **IMPERTINENCE**. HE SEIZED A TUREEN OF **HOT APPLE SAUCE**, AND...

SPOOSH

AAAGGH!

MR. EARNSHAW SNATCHED UP THE CULPRIT **DIRECTLY** AND CONVEYED HIM TO HIS **CHAMBER**; WHERE, DOUBTLESS, HE ADMINISTERED A **ROUGH** REMEDY TO **COOL** THE FIT OF **PASSION**.

I PERCEIVED THAT CATHY WAS IN *PURGATORY* THROUGHOUT THE DAY, AND *WEARYING* TO FIND AN OPPORTUNITY OF PAYING A VISIT TO HEATHCLIFF, WHO HAD BEEN *LOCKED UP* BY THE MASTER.

WHEN I WENT UP TO SEE HEATHCLIFF I HEARD *HER* VOICE WITHIN.

THE LITTLE MONKEY HAD CREPT BY THE SKYLIGHT OF *ONE* GARRET, ALONG THE *ROOF*, INTO THE SKYLIGHT OF THE *OTHER*, AND IT WAS WITH THE UTMOST DIFFICULTY I COULD COAX HER *OUT* AGAIN.

WHEN SHE DID COME, HEATHCLIFF CAME *WITH* HER, AND SHE *INSISTED* THAT I SHOULD TAKE HIM INTO THE KITCHEN, AS MY FELLOW-SERVANT HAD GONE TO A NEIGHBOUR'S, TO BE *REMOVED* FROM THE SOUND OF OUR "DEVIL'S PSALMODY", AS IT *PLEASED* HIM TO *CALL IT.* I TOLD THEM I INTENDED BY NO MEANS TO *ENCOURAGE* THEIR TRICKS; BUT AS THE PRISONER HAD NEVER BROKEN HIS FAST SINCE *YESTERDAY'S* DINNER, I WOULD WINK AT HIS CHEATING MR. HINDLEY THAT *ONCE.*

WHAT ARE *YOU* THINKING OF?

I'M TRYING TO SETTLE HOW I SHALL PAY HINDLEY *BACK.* I DON'T CARE HOW LONG I WAIT, IF I CAN ONLY DO IT AT *LAST.*

I HOPE *HE* WILL NOT *DIE* BEFORE I DO!

FOR *SHAME*, HEATHCLIFF! IT IS FOR GOD TO PUNISH *WICKED* PEOPLE; WE SHOULD LEARN TO FORGIVE.

NO, GOD *WON'T* HAVE THE *SATISFACTION* THAT I SHALL.

I ONLY WISH I KNEW THE *BEST* WAY! LET ME *ALONE*, AND I'LL *PLAN* IT OUT:

WHILE I'M THINKING OF *THAT* I DON'T FEEL PAIN.

37

CHAPTER VIII

ON THE MORNING OF A FINE JUNE DAY IN 1778, MY *FIRST* BONNY LITTLE *NURSLING,* AND THE *LAST* OF THE ANCIENT EARNSHAW STOCK, WAS *BORN.*

WE WERE BUSY WITH THE *HAY* IN A FAR AWAY FIELD WHEN I WAS CALLED *HOME.* THE DOCTOR SAID MRS. HINDLEY WAS *ILL* AND WOULD BE *DEAD* BEFORE *WINTER.*

HOW IS THE BABY?

NEARLY READY TO *RUN ABOUT,* NELL!

AND THE *MISTRESS?* THE DOCTOR SAYS SHE'S --

DAMN THE DOCTOR!

FRANCES IS *QUITE* RIGHT: SHE'LL BE PERFECTLY *WELL* BY THIS TIME NEXT WEEK.

ARE YOU GOING UP-STAIRS? TELL HER THAT I'LL COME, IF SHE'LL PROMISE NOT TO *TALK.* MR. KENNETH SAYS SHE MUST BE *QUIET.*

I *DELIVERED* THIS MESSAGE...

I HARDLY SPOKE A *WORD,* ELLEN, AND THERE HE HAS GONE OUT TWICE, *CRYING.*

WELL, SAY I PROMISE I WON'T *SPEAK:*

BUT THAT DOES NOT BIND ME NOT TO *LAUGH* AT HIM!

POOR SOUL! TILL WITHIN A *WEEK* OF HER *DEATH* THAT GAY HEART NEVER *FAILED* HER; AND HER HUSBAND *PERSISTED* DOGGEDLY, NAY, *FURIOUSLY,* IN AFFIRMING HER HEALTH *IMPROVED* EVERY DAY.

BUT ONE NIGHT, WHILE LEANING ON HIS SHOULDER, IN THE ACT OF SAYING SHE THOUGHT SHE SHOULD BE ABLE TO *GET UP* TO-MORROW, A FIT OF *COUGHING* TOOK HER – A VERY *SLIGHT* ONE – HE RAISED HER IN HIS *ARMS;* SHE PUT HER TWO HANDS ABOUT HIS NECK, HER FACE *CHANGED...*

38

...AND SHE WAS **DEAD**.

HINDLEY GREW **DESPERATE** AFTER THAT: HIS **SORROW** WAS OF THAT KIND THAT WILL **NOT** LAMENT. HE NEITHER **WEPT** NOR **PRAYED**; HE CURSED AND DEFIED: EXECRATED **GOD** AND **MAN,** AND GAVE HIMSELF UP TO **RECKLESS** DISSIPATION.

THE SERVANTS COULD NOT **BEAR** HIS TYRANNICAL AND **EVIL** CONDUCT LONG: JOSEPH AND I WERE THE **ONLY** TWO THAT WOULD **STAY**.

THE MASTER'S BAD WAYS AND BAD **COMPANIONS** FORMED A **PRETTY** EXAMPLE FOR CATHERINE AND HEATHCLIFF. HIS **TREATMENT** OF THE LATTER WAS ENOUGH TO MAKE A **FIEND** OF A **SAINT**.

THWAK

AND, TRULY, IT APPEARED AS IF THE LAD WERE **POSSESSED** OF SOMETHING **DIABOLICAL** AT THAT PERIOD. HE **DELIGHTED** TO WITNESS HINDLEY DEGRADING HIMSELF **PAST** REDEMPTION; AND BECAME **DAILY** MORE NOTABLE FOR SAVAGE **SULLENNESS** AND **FEROCITY**. I COULD NOT **HALF** TELL WHAT AN **INFERNAL** HOUSE WE HAD.

BY THE TIME HEATHCLIFF HAD REACHED THE AGE OF *SIXTEEN*, HE HAD *LOST* THE BENEFIT OF HIS EARLY *EDUCATION*:

CONTINUAL HARD WORK, BEGUN *SOON* AND CONCLUDED *LATE*, HAD EXTINGUISHED ANY CURIOSITY HE *ONCE* POSSESSED IN *PURSUIT* OF *KNOWLEDGE*, AND ANY LOVE FOR *BOOKS* OR *LEARNING*.

CATHERINE AND HE WERE CONSTANT COMPANIONS *STILL* AT HIS SEASONS OF *RESPITE* FROM LABOUR; BUT HE HAD *CEASED* TO EXPRESS HIS FONDNESS FOR HER IN WORDS, AND RECOILED WITH ANGRY *SUSPICION* FROM HER GIRLISH *CARESSES*.

CATHY, ARE YOU *BUSY* THIS AFTERNOON? ARE YOU *GOING* ANYWHERE?

NO, IT IS RAINING.

WHY HAVE YOU THAT *SILK* FROCK ON, THEN? NOBODY COMING *HERE*, I HOPE?

NOT THAT I *KNOW* OF; BUT YOU SHOULD BE IN THE *FIELD* NOW, HEATHCLIFF. IT IS AN *HOUR* PAST DINNER TIME: I THOUGHT YOU WERE *GONE*.

I'LL NOT WORK ANY *MORE* TO-DAY: I'LL SIT WITH *YOU*.

SHOULD I *ALWAYS* BE SITTING WITH *YOU?* WHAT *GOOD* DO I GET? WHAT DO YOU *TALK* ABOUT?

YOU MIGHT BE *DUMB*, OR A *BABY*, FOR ANYTHING YOU SAY TO *AMUSE* ME, OR FOR ANYTHING YOU *DO*, EITHER!

YOU NEVER TOLD ME *BEFORE* THAT I TALKED TOO *LITTLE*, OR THAT YOU DISLIKED MY *COMPANY*, CATHY!

IT'S *NO* COMPANY AT *ALL*, WHEN PEOPLE KNOW NOTHING AND *SAY* NOTHING.

knock knock

YOU'VE MADE ME **AFRAID** AND **ASHAMED** OF YOU. I'LL **NOT** COME HERE AGAIN!

AND YOU TOLD A **DELIBERATE** UNTRUTH!

I DIDN'T! I DID **NOTHING** DELIBERATELY.

WELL, GO, IF YOU PLEASE – GET **AWAY**!

AND NOW I'LL **CRY** – I'LL CRY MYSELF **SICK**!

≥SOB≤

≥SOB≤

MISS IS **DREADFULLY** WAYWARD, SIR. AS **BAD** AS ANY MARRED **CHILD**:

YOU'D BETTER BE RIDING **HOME**, OR ELSE SHE **WILL** BE SICK, ONLY TO GRIEVE US.

≥SOB≤

≥SOB≤

THE SOFT THING LOOKED ASKANCE: HE POSSESSED THE POWER TO **DEPART** AS MUCH AS A **CAT** POSSESSES THE POWER TO LEAVE A **MOUSE** HALF KILLED, OR A **BIRD** HALF EATEN.

AH, I THOUGHT, THERE WILL BE NO **SAVING** HIM. HE'S **DOOMED**, AND **FLIES** TO HIS FATE!

43

CHAPTER IX

A-HA — *Z#!

MR. HINDLEY'S ARRIVAL DROVE LINTON TO HIS *HORSE,* AND CATHERINE TO HER *CHAMBER.*

HE CAUGHT ME IN THE ACT OF STOWING AWAY HIS *SON.* THE POOR THING REMAINED PERFECTLY *QUIET WHEREVER I* CHOSE TO PUT HIM.

THERE, I'VE FOUND IT *OUT* AT LAST!

BY HEAVEN AND HELL, YOU'VE SWORN BETWEEN YOU TO *MURDER* THAT CHILD!

I *KNOW* HOW IT IS, NOW, THAT HE IS *ALWAYS* OUT OF MY WAY.

BUT, WITH THE HELP OF *SATAN,* I SHALL MAKE YOU *SWALLOW* THE *CARVING-KNIFE,* NELLY!

I DON'T *LIKE* THE CARVING-KNIFE, MR. HINDLEY. IT HAS BEEN CUTTING RED *HERRINGS.* I'D RATHER BE *SHOT,* IF YOU PLEASE.

WAAAAH!

NO *LAW* IN ENGLAND CAN *HINDER* A MAN FROM KEEPING HIS HOUSE DECENT, AND MINE'S *ABOMINABLE!*

PTOO

IT TASTES DETESTABLE. I WILL *NOT* TAKE IT ON *ANY* ACCOUNT.

45

HEATHCLIFF ARRIVED UNDERNEATH...

AHAAAII!

...JUST AT THE *CRITICAL* MOMENT;

BY A NATURAL IMPULSE...

WAAAH!

...HE ARRESTED HIS *DESCENT*...

...AND LOOKED UP TO SEE THE *AUTHOR* OF THE *ACCIDENT.*

HIS *FACE* EXPRESSED, IN PLAINER THAN *WORDS* COULD DO, THE INTENSEST *ANGUISH* AT HAVING MADE HIMSELF THE INSTRUMENT OF *THWARTING* HIS OWN *REVENGE.*

HAD IT BEEN *DARK,* I DARESAY HE WOULD HAVE TRIED TO *REMEDY* THE MISTAKE BY *SMASHING* HARETON'S SKULL ON THE STEPS; BUT, WE WITNESSED HIS *SALVATION.*

WAAAH!

WAAAH!

IT IS YOUR FAULT, ELLEN. YOU SHOULD HAVE KEPT HIM OUT OF SIGHT. IS HE INJURED?

INJURED! OH, I WONDER HIS MOTHER DOES NOT RISE FROM HER GRAVE.

WAAAH!

HE HATES YOU – THEY ALL HATE YOU – THAT'S THE TRUTH! A HAPPY FAMILY YOU HAVE; AND A PRETTY STATE YOU'RE COME TO!

I WAS PRESENTLY BELOW WITH MY PRECIOUS CHARGE PRESSED TO MY HEART. HINDLEY DESCENDED MORE LEISURELY, SOBERED AND ABASHED.

I SHALL COME TO A PRETTIER, YET, NELLY. AT PRESENT, CONVEY YOURSELF AND HIM AWAY.

AND HARK YOU, HEATHCLIFF! CLEAR YOU TOO, QUITE FROM MY REACH AND HEARING. I WOULDN'T MURDER YOU TO-NIGHT; UNLESS, PERHAPS, I SET THE HOUSE ON FIRE:

BUT THAT'S AS MY FANCY GOES.

It's a pity he cannot kill himself with drink.

He's doing his very utmost; but his constitution defies him.

47

I WENT INTO THE KITCHEN, AND SAT DOWN TO LULL MY LITTLE LAMB TO *SLEEP*.

ARE YOU *ALONE*, NELLY?

YES, MISS.

WHERE'S HEATHCLIFF?

ABOUT HIS WORK IN THE *STABLE*.

NELLY, WILL YOU KEEP A *SECRET* FOR ME?

IS IT WORTH KEEPING?

YES, AND IT *WORRIES* ME, AND I *MUST* LET IT *OUT!* I WANT TO KNOW WHAT I SHOULD *DO*.

TO-DAY, EDGAR LINTON HAS ASKED ME TO *MARRY* HIM, AND I'VE GIVEN HIM AN *ANSWER*.

NOW, BEFORE I TELL YOU WHETHER IT WAS A *CONSENT* OR *DENIAL*, YOU TELL ME WHICH IT *OUGHT* TO HAVE BEEN.

REALLY, MISS CATHERINE, HOW CAN I KNOW?

TO BE SURE, CONSIDERING THE *EXHIBITION* YOU PERFORMED IN HIS PRESENCE THIS AFTERNOON, I MIGHT SAY IT WOULD BE WISE TO *REFUSE* HIM:

SINCE HE ASKED YOU *AFTER* THAT, HE MUST EITHER BE HOPELESSLY *STUPID* OR A VENTURESOME *FOOL*.

IF YOU TALK SO, I *WON'T* TELL YOU ANY *MORE!*

I ACCEPTED HIM, NELLY. BE *QUICK*, AND SAY WHETHER I WAS *WRONG!*

YOU *ACCEPTED* HIM! THEN WHAT GOOD IS IT *DISCUSSING* THE MATTER? YOU HAVE PLEDGED YOUR *WORD* AND CANNOT *RETRACT*.

BUT, SAY WHETHER I *SHOULD* HAVE DONE SO – *DO!*

48

THERE ARE MANY THINGS TO BE CONSIDERED BEFORE THAT QUESTION CAN BE ANSWERED PROPERLY.

FIRST AND FOREMOST, DO YOU LOVE MR. EDGAR?

WHO CAN HELP IT? OF COURSE I DO

WHY DO YOU LOVE HIM, MISS CATHY?

WELL, BECAUSE HE IS HANDSOME, AND PLEASANT TO BE WITH.

BAD!

AND BECAUSE HE IS YOUNG AND CHEERFUL.

BAD, STILL.

AND BECAUSE HE LOVES ME.

INDIFFERENT, COMING THERE.

AND HE WILL BE RICH, AND I SHALL LIKE TO BE THE GREATEST WOMAN OF THE NEIGHBOURHOOD, AND I SHALL BE PROUD OF HAVING SUCH A HUSBAND.

WORST OF ALL.

YOUR BROTHER WILL BE PLEASED; THE OLD LADY AND GENTLEMAN WILL NOT OBJECT, I THINK; YOU WILL ESCAPE FROM A DISORDERLY, COMFORTLESS HOME INTO A WEALTHY, RESPECTABLE ONE; AND YOU LOVE EDGAR, AND EDGAR LOVES YOU.

ALL SEEMS SMOOTH AND EASY: WHERE IS THE OBSTACLE?

49

HERE!

AND HERE!

IN WHICHEVER PLACE THE **SOUL** LIVES. IN MY SOUL AND IN MY **HEART**, I'M CONVINCED I'M **WRONG!**

I'VE DREAMT IN MY LIFE DREAMS THAT HAVE **STAYED** WITH ME EVER AFTER, AND **CHANGED** MY IDEAS:

THEY'VE GONE THROUGH AND **THROUGH** ME, LIKE WINE THROUGH WATER, AND ALTERED THE **COLOUR** OF MY **MIND.**

AND **THIS** IS ONE: I'M GOING TO **TELL** IT – BUT TAKE CARE NOT TO **SMILE** AT ANY PART OF IT.

IF I WERE IN **HEAVEN,** NELLY, I SHOULD BE EXTREMELY **MISERABLE.** I **DREAMT** ONCE THAT I WAS THERE.

HEAVEN DID NOT SEEM TO BE MY **HOME;** AND I BROKE MY HEART WITH **WEEPING** TO COME **BACK** TO EARTH; AND THE **ANGELS** WERE SO **ANGRY** THAT THEY **FLUNG** ME OUT INTO THE MIDDLE OF THE **HEATH** ON THE TOP OF WUTHERING HEIGHTS; WHERE I WOKE **SOBBING** FOR JOY.

THAT WILL DO TO EXPLAIN MY **SECRET,** AS WELL AS THE OTHER.

I'VE NO MORE BUSINESS TO **MARRY** EDGAR LINTON THAN I HAVE TO BE IN **HEAVEN;**

AND IF THE **WICKED** MAN IN THERE HAD NOT BROUGHT HEATHCLIFF SO **LOW,** I SHOULDN'T HAVE **THOUGHT** OF IT.

IT WOULD **DEGRADE** ME TO MARRY **HEATHCLIFF** NOW.

SO HE SHALL **NEVER** KNOW HOW I **LOVE HIM:** AND THAT, NOT BECAUSE HE'S **HANDSOME,** NELLY, BUT BECAUSE HE'S **MORE** MYSELF THAN I AM.

WHATEVER OUR SOULS ARE MADE OF, HIS AND MINE ARE THE SAME; AND LINTON'S IS AS DIFFERENT AS A MOONBEAM FROM LIGHTNING, OR FROST FROM FIRE.

ERE THIS SPEECH ENDED, I BECAME SENSIBLE OF HEATHCLIFF'S PRESENCE. HAVING NOTICED A SLIGHT MOVEMENT, I TURNED MY HEAD, AND SAW HIM RISE AND STEAL OUT NOISELESSLY.

HUSH!

WHY?

JOSEPH IS HERE, AND HEATHCLIFF WILL COME IN WITH HIM. I'M NOT SURE WHETHER HE WERE NOT AT THE DOOR THIS MOMENT.

OH, HE COULDN'T OVERHEAR ME AT THE DOOR!

AS SOON AS YOU BECOME MRS. LINTON, HEATHCLIFF LOSES FRIENDS, AND LOVE, AND ALL!

HAVE YOU CONSIDERED HOW YOU'LL BEAR THE SEPARATION, AND HOW HE'LL BEAR TO BE QUITE DESERTED IN THE WORLD?

WHO IS TO SEPARATE US, PRAY? THEY'LL MEET THE FATE OF MILO! NOT AS LONG AS I LIVE, ELLEN: FOR NO MORTAL CREATURE.

EVERY LINTON ON THE FACE OF THE EARTH MIGHT MELT INTO NOTHING BEFORE I COULD CONSENT TO FORSAKE HEATHCLIFF.

OH, THAT'S NOT WHAT I INTEND – THAT'S NOT WHAT I MEAN! I SHOULDN'T BE MRS. LINTON WERE SUCH A PRICE DEMANDED!

HE'LL BE AS MUCH TO ME AS HE HAS BEEN ALL HIS LIFETIME.

NELLY, I SEE NOW, YOU THINK ME A SELFISH WRETCH; BUT DID IT NEVER STRIKE YOU THAT IF HEATHCLIFF AND I MARRIED, WE SHOULD BE BEGGARS? WHEREAS, IF I MARRY LINTON, I CAN AID HEATHCLIFF TO RISE, AND PLACE HIM OUT OF MY BROTHER'S POWER.

WITH YOUR **HUSBAND'S** MONEY, MISS CATHERINE?

YOU'LL FIND HIM NOT SO **PLIABLE** AS YOU CALCULATE UPON: AND, THOUGH I'M HARDLY A JUDGE, I THINK THAT'S THE **WORST** MOTIVE YOU'VE GIVEN **YET** FOR BEING THE **WIFE** OF YOUNG LINTON.

IT IS **NOT** -- IT IS THE BEST! SURELY YOU AND EVERYBODY HAVE A **NOTION** THAT THERE IS AN EXISTENCE OF YOURS **BEYOND** YOU.

MY GREAT **MISERIES** IN THIS WORLD HAVE BEEN **HEATHCLIFF'S** MISERIES, AND I **WATCHED** AND FELT EACH FROM THE BEGINNING: MY GREAT THOUGHT IN **LIVING** IS **HIMSELF.**

IF ALL **ELSE** PERISHED, AND **HE** REMAINED, I SHOULD STILL **CONTINUE** TO BE; AND IF ALL ELSE **REMAINED,** AND **HE** WERE ANNIHILATED, THE UNIVERSE WOULD TURN TO A MIGHTY **STRANGER:** I SHOULD NOT SEEM A **PART** OF IT.

NELLY, I **AM** HEATHCLIFF! HE'S ALWAYS, **ALWAYS** IN MY MIND: **NOT** AS A PLEASURE, ANY MORE THAN I AM ALWAYS A PLEASURE TO MYSELF, BUT AS MY OWN **BEING.** SO **DON'T** TALK OF OUR **SEPARATION** AGAIN: IT IS **IMPRACTICABLE** AND --

--

UND HAH ISN'T THAT **NOWT** COMED IN FROUGH TH' **FIELD,** BE THIS TIME?

WHAT IS HE ABOUT? GIRT **IDLE** SEEGHT!

I'LL **CALL** HIM. HE'S IN THE **BARN,** I'VE NO DOUBT.

I WENT AND *CALLED*, BUT GOT NO *ANSWER.*

HAVE YOU *FOUND* HEATHCLIFF, YOU *ASS?* HAVE YOU BEEN *LOOKING* FOR HIM, AS I *ORDERED?*

AW SUD *MORE* LIKKER LOOK FOR TH' *HORSE.* IT 'UD BE TUH MORE *SENSE.*

BUD, AW CAN LOOK FOR *NORTHER* HORSE, NUR MAN UF A NEEGHT LOIKE *THIS* – AS *BLACK* AS T'*CHIMBLEY!* UND HEATHCLIFF'S NOAN T' CHAP TUH COOM UT MAW WHISTLE – HAPPEN HE'LL BE *LESS* HARD UH HEARING WI' *YE!*

MISTRESS *COMMANDED* JOSEPH THAT HE MUST RUN DOWN THE ROAD, AND, *WHEREVER* HEATHCLIFF HAD RAMBLED, *FIND* AND MAKE HIM RE-ENTER *DIRECTLY!*

IT WAS A VERY *DARK* EVENING FOR SUMMER.

HEATHCLIFF! HEATHCLIFF!

CATHERINE WOULD NOT BE *PERSUADED* INTO TRANQUILLITY. SHE KEPT WANDERING TO AND FRO, FROM THE GATE TO THE DOOR, IN A STATE OF *AGITATION* WHICH PERMITTED NO *REPOSE;*

HEEDLESS OF MY EXPOSTULATIONS AND THE GROWLING *THUNDER,* AND THE GREAT *DROPS* THAT BEGAN TO PLASH AROUND HER, SHE REMAINED, *CALLING* AT INTERVALS...

HEATHCLIFF!

HEATHCLIFF!

...AND THEN LISTENING...

...AND THEN CRYING *OUTRIGHT.*

WELL, MISS! YOU ARE NOT BENT ON GETTING YOUR *DEATH,* ARE YOU?

DO YOU *KNOW* WHAT O'CLOCK IT IS? HALF-PAST *TWELVE.* COME, COME TO *BED!*

THERE'S NO USE *WAITING* ANY LONGER ON THAT *FOOLISH* BOY: HE'LL BE GONE TO *GIMMERTON,* AND HE'LL *STAY* THERE NOW.

ABOUT *MIDNIGHT,* THE STORM CAME RATTLING OVER THE HEIGHTS IN FULL *FURY.*

HE GUESSES WE *SHOULDN'T* WAIT FOR HIM TILL THIS *LATE* HOUR: AT LEAST HE GUESSES THAT ONLY *MR. HINDLEY* WOULD BE *UP;*

AND HE'D RATHER *AVOID* HAVING THE DOOR *OPENED* BY THE MASTER.

CRAAACK

CRAAASH

I BETOOK MYSELF TO BED WITH LITTLE HARETON, WHO SLEPT AS FAST AS IF EVERY ONE HAD BEEN SLEEPING ROUND HIM.

COMING DOWN SOMEWHAT *LATER* THAN USUAL, I SAW, BY THE SUNBEAMS PIERCING THE CHINKS OF THE SHUTTERS, MISS CATHERINE *STILL SEATED* NEAR THE FIREPLACE.

HINDLEY STOOD ON THE KITCHEN HEARTH, HAGGARD AND *DROWSY*.

WHAT *AILS* YOU, CATHY? YOU LOOK AS *DISMAL* AS A DROWNED WHELP.

I'VE BEEN *WET*, AND I'M *COLD*, THAT'S ALL.

OH, SHE *IS* NAUGHTY! SHE GOT *STEEPED* IN THE *SHOWER* OF YESTERDAY EVENING.

SHE'S ILL. I SUPPOSE *THAT'S* THE REASON SHE WOULD NOT GO TO BED.

DAMN IT! I DON'T WANT TO BE TROUBLED WITH *MORE* SICKNESS HERE. GET TO YOUR *ROOM*.

I SHALL NEVER FORGET WHAT A *SCENE* SHE ACTED WHEN WE REACHED HER CHAMBER: IT *TERRIFIED* ME.

GRRRAAARGH!

PERHAPS HE'S *GONE*.

AAALGH!

I THOUGHT SHE WAS GOING *MAD*, AND I *BEGGED* JOSEPH TO RUN FOR THE *DOCTOR*.

IT PROVED THE COMMENCEMENT OF *DELIRIUM*: MR. KENNETH, AS SOON AS HE SAW HER, PRONOUNCED HER *DANGEROUSLY* ILL; SHE HAD A *FEVER*.

SHE WEATHERED IT *THROUGH*. OLD MRS. LINTON PAID US *SEVERAL VISITS*, TO BE SURE, AND SET THINGS TO RIGHTS, AND *SCOLDED* AND ORDERED US ALL;

AND WHEN CATHERINE WAS *CONVALESCENT*, SHE *INSISTED* ON CONVEYING HER TO THRUSHCROSS GRANGE: FOR WHICH DELIVERANCE WE WERE VERY *GRATEFUL*.

BUT THE POOR DAME HAD REASON TO *REPENT* OF HER *KINDNESS*: SHE AND HER HUSBAND *BOTH* TOOK THE *FEVER*, AND *DIED* WITHIN A FEW DAYS OF EACH OTHER.

OUR YOUNG LADY *RETURNED* TO US *SAUCIER* AND *MORE* PASSIONATE, AND *HAUGHTIER* THAN EVER.

HEATHCLIFF HAD NEVER BEEN *HEARD* OF SINCE THE *EVENING* OF THE *THUNDER STORM*; AND, ONE DAY, I HAD THE *MISFORTUNE*, WHEN SHE PROVOKED ME *EXCEEDINGLY*, TO LAY THE *BLAME* OF HIS DISAPPEARANCE ON HER: WHERE INDEED IT BELONGED, AS SHE WELL *KNEW*.

FROM THAT PERIOD, FOR *SEVERAL* MONTHS, SHE *CEASED* TO HOLD *ANY* COMMUNICATION WITH ME.

MR. EARNSHAW ALLOWED CATHERINE **WHATEVER** SHE PLEASED TO **DEMAND;** NOT FROM **AFFECTION,** BUT FROM **PRIDE:** HE WISHED EARNESTLY TO SEE HER BRING **HONOUR** TO THE FAMILY BY AN **ALLIANCE** WITH THE LINTONS.

EDGAR LINTON, AS **MULTITUDES** HAVE BEEN **BEFORE** AND WILL BE **AFTER** HIM, WAS **INFATUATED;** AND BELIEVED HIMSELF THE **HAPPIEST** MAN ALIVE ON THE DAY HE LED CATHERINE TO GIMMERTON **CHAPEL,** THREE YEARS SUBSEQUENT TO HIS FATHER'S DEATH.

MUCH AGAINST MY INCLINATION, I WAS PERSUADED TO **LEAVE** WUTHERING HEIGHTS AND ACCOMPANY HER **HERE** TO THE GRANGE.

LITTLE HARETON WAS NEARLY **FIVE** YEARS OLD, AND I HAD JUST **BEGUN** TO TEACH HIM HIS LETTERS. WE MADE A **SAD** PARTING.

SINCE THEN HE HAS BEEN A **STRANGER:** AND IT'S VERY QUEER TO **THINK** IT, BUT I'VE NO DOUBT HE HAS COMPLETELY **FORGOTTEN** ALL ABOUT ELLEN DEAN, AND THAT HE WAS **EVER** MORE THAN ALL THE **WORLD** TO HER, AND **SHE** TO HIM!

AT THIS POINT OF THE HOUSEKEEPER'S STORY, SHE CHANCED TO GLANCE TOWARDS THE **TIME-PIECE** OVER THE CHIMNEY: **HALF-PAST ONE.** SHE WOULD NOT **HEAR** OF STAYING A SECOND LONGER: IN TRUTH, I FELT RATHER DISPOSED TO **DEFER** THE **SEQUEL** OF HER NARRATIVE MYSELF.

A *CHARMING* INTRODUCTION TO A HERMIT'S LIFE! FOUR WEEKS' *TORTURE* AND *SICKNESS!* WHY NOT HAVE UP *MRS. DEAN* TO *FINISH* HER TALE?

I CAN RECOLLECT ITS *CHIEF* INCIDENTS. I REMEMBER HER *HERO* HAD *RUN OFF,* AND NEVER BEEN HEARD OF FOR THREE YEARS; AND THE *HEROINE* WAS *MARRIED.* I'LL RING.

CHAPTER X

NOW *CONTINUE* THE STORY OF MR. HEATHCLIFF FROM WHERE YOU LEFT OFF TO THE *PRESENT* DAY.

I GOT MISS CATHERINE AND MYSELF TO THRUSHCROSS GRANGE; AND, TO MY *AGREEABLE* DISAPPOINTMENT, SHE BEHAVED *INFINITELY* BETTER THAN I DARED TO *EXPECT.* SHE SEEMED ALMOST *OVER* FOND OF MR. LINTON; AND EVEN TO HIS *SISTER,* SHE SHOWED PLENTY OF *AFFECTION.* THEY WERE BOTH VERY *ATTENTIVE* TO HER COMFORT, CERTAINLY.

CATHERINE HAD SEASONS OF *GLOOM* AND *SILENCE,* NOW AND THEN; THEY WERE *RESPECTED* WITH *SYMPATHISING* SILENCE BY HER *HUSBAND.*

THE RETURN OF SUNSHINE WAS *WELCOMED* BY *ANSWERING* SUNSHINE FROM HIM. I BELIEVE I MAY ASSERT THAT THEY WERE *REALLY* IN POSSESSION OF DEEP AND GROWING *HAPPINESS.*

IT *ENDED.* WELL, WE MUST BE FOR *OURSELVES* IN THE LONG RUN; AND IT ENDED WHEN CIRCUMSTANCES CAUSED EACH TO FEEL THAT THE *ONE'S* INTEREST WAS NOT THE CHIEF CONSIDERATION IN THE *OTHER'S* THOUGHTS.

ON A *MELLOW* EVENING IN SEPTEMBER, I WAS COMING FROM THE GARDEN WITH A HEAVY BASKET OF *APPLES* WHICH I HAD BEEN GATHERING.

NELLY, IS THAT *YOU?*

MR. *EARNSHAW?* OH, NO! THE VOICE HAS *NO* RESEMBLANCE TO *HIS.*

I HAVE WAITED HERE AN *HOUR,* AND THE *WHOLE* OF THAT TIME ALL ROUND HAS BEEN AS STILL AS *DEATH.*

I DARED NOT *ENTER.* YOU DO NOT *KNOW* ME?

A PERSON FROM GIMMERTON WISHES TO **SEE** YOU, MA'AM.

WHAT DOES HE WANT?

I DIDN'T **QUESTION** HIM.

WHO IS IT, NELLY?

SOME ONE MISTRESS DOES NOT **EXPECT**. THAT HEATHCLIFF – YOU RECOLLECT HIM, SIR – WHO USED TO LIVE AT MR. **EARNSHAW'S**.

WHAT?

THE **GIPSY** – THE **PLOUGHBOY?** WHY DID YOU NOT **SAY** SO TO CATHERINE?

?!?

OH, EDGAR, **DARLING!** HEATHCLIFF'S COME **BACK** – HE IS!

WELL, DON'T **STRANGLE** ME FOR THAT! HE NEVER STRUCK ME AS SUCH A **MARVELLOUS TREASURE.** THERE IS NO NEED TO BE FRANTIC.

I KNOW YOU DIDN'T **LIKE** HIM. YET, FOR **MY** SAKE, YOU MUST BE **FRIENDS** NOW.

SHALL I TELL HIM TO COME UP?

HERE? INTO THE PARLOUR?

WHERE ELSE?

CATHERINE, **TRY** TO BE **GLAD,** WITHOUT BEING **ABSURD!** THE WHOLE **HOUSEHOLD** NEED NOT **WITNESS** THE SIGHT OF YOUR WELCOMING A RUNAWAY **SERVANT** AS A **BROTHER.**

THE LADY'S CHEEKS *GLOWED* WHEN HER *FRIEND* APPEARED AT THE DOOR.

SHE LED HIM TO LINTON; AND THEN SHE *SEIZED* LINTON'S *RELUCTANT* FINGERS AND CRUSHED THEM INTO HIS.

NOW *FULLY* REVEALED BY THE FIRE AND CANDLELIGHT, I WAS *AMAZED*, MORE THAN EVER, TO BEHOLD THE *TRANSFORMATION* OF HEATHCLIFF.

HE HAD GROWN A TALL, ATHLETIC, WELL-FORMED *MAN;* BESIDE WHOM MY *MASTER* SEEMED QUITE SLENDER AND *YOUTH-LIKE*.

HIS *UPRIGHT* CARRIAGE *SUGGESTED* THE IDEA OF HIS HAVING BEEN IN THE *ARMY*. HIS COUNTENANCE WAS MUCH *OLDER* IN EXPRESSION AND DECISION OF FEATURE THAN MR. LINTON'S; IT LOOKED *INTELLIGENT,* AND RETAINED NO MARKS OF FORMER *DEGRADATION.*

A HALF-CIVILISED *FEROCITY* LURKED YET IN THE DEPRESSED BROWS AND EYES FULL OF BLACK *FIRE,* BUT IT WAS *SUBDUED;* AND HIS MANNER WAS EVEN *DIGNIFIED;* QUITE DIVESTED OF *ROUGHNESS,* THOUGH TOO STERN FOR *GRACE.*

MY MASTER'S SURPRISE EQUALLED OR *EXCEEDED* MINE: HE REMAINED FOR A MINUTE AT A *LOSS* HOW TO ADDRESS THE PLOUGHBOY, AS HE HAD CALLED HIM. HEATHCLIFF *DROPPED* HIS SLIGHT HAND, AND STOOD LOOKING AT HIM COOLLY TILL HE CHOSE TO *SPEAK*.

SIT DOWN, SIR.

MRS. LINTON, RECALLING **OLD** TIMES, WOULD HAVE ME GIVE YOU A **CORDIAL** RECEPTION; AND, OF COURSE, I AM GRATIFIED WHEN **ANYTHING** OCCURS TO **PLEASE** HER.

AND I **ALSO**, ESPECIALLY IF IT BE ANYTHING IN WHICH I HAVE A **PART**.

I SHALL STAY AN **HOUR** OR TWO WILLINGLY.

I SHALL THINK IT A **DREAM** TO-MORROW! I SHALL NOT BE ABLE TO **BELIEVE** THAT I HAVE SEEN, AND TOUCHED, AND **SPOKEN** TO YOU ONCE MORE.

AND YET, *CRUEL HEATHCLIFF!* YOU DON'T **DESERVE** THIS WELCOME. TO BE ABSENT AND SILENT FOR **THREE** YEARS, AND **NEVER** TO **THINK** OF ME!

A LITTLE **MORE** THAN **YOU** HAVE THOUGHT OF **ME**. NAY, YOU'LL **NOT** DRIVE ME OFF **AGAIN**.

YOU WERE **REALLY** SORRY FOR ME, WERE YOU? WELL, THERE WAS A **CAUSE**. I'VE FOUGHT THROUGH A **BITTER** LIFE SINCE I LAST HEARD YOUR VOICE;

AND YOU MUST **FORGIVE** ME, FOR I STRUGGLED **ONLY** FOR YOU!

CATHERINE, UNLESS WE ARE TO HAVE COLD TEA, PLEASE TO COME TO THE **TABLE**.

MR. HEATHCLIFF WILL HAVE A **LONG** WALK, WHEREVER HE MAY LODGE TO-NIGHT; AND I'M **THIRSTY**.

THEIR GUEST DID NOT PROTRACT HIS STAY THAT EVENING ABOVE AN HOUR LONGER.

THAT NIGHT, MRS. LINTON COULD NOT SLEEP THROUGH *HAPPINESS*, AND GLIDED INTO MY CHAMBER. SHE TOLD ME MR. LINTON WAS *SULKY*. I ADVISED CATHERINE TO VALUE MR. LINTON THE **MORE** FOR HIS *AFFECTION*.

IN SELF-COMPLACENT CONVICTION SHE DEPARTED FROM ME TO MAKE HER *PEACE* WITH HER HUSBAND.

THE *SUCCESS* OF HER *FULFILLED* RESOLUTION WAS *OBVIOUS* ON THE MORROW: MR. LINTON HAD NOT ONLY *ABJURED* HIS PEEVISHNESS, BUT HE VENTURED NO *OBJECTION* TO HER TAKING *ISABELLA* WITH HER TO WUTHERING HEIGHTS, WHERE HEATHCLIFF WAS *LODGED*, IN THE AFTERNOON;

AND SHE *REWARDED* HIM WITH SUCH A *SUMMER* OF SWEETNESS AND *AFFECTION* IN RETURN AS MADE THE HOUSE A *PARADISE* FOR SEVERAL DAYS; *BOTH* MASTER AND SERVANTS *PROFITING* FROM THE PERPETUAL *SUNSHINE*.

HEATHCLIFF – **MR. HEATHCLIFF** I SHOULD SAY IN FUTURE – USED THE LIBERTY OF *VISITING* AT THRUSHCROSS GRANGE *CAUTIOUSLY*, AT FIRST: HE SEEMED ESTIMATING HOW FAR ITS *OWNER* WOULD *BEAR* HIS *INTRUSION*.

CATHERINE, ALSO, DEEMED IT JUDICIOUS TO *MODERATE* HER EXPRESSIONS OF PLEASURE IN *RECEIVING* HIM; AND HE GRADUALLY ESTABLISHED HIS RIGHT TO BE *EXPECTED*.

MY MASTER'S NEW SOURCE OF *TROUBLE* SPRANG FROM THE *NOT ANTICIPATED* MISFORTUNE OF *ISABELLA* LINTON EVINCING A SUDDEN AND *IRRESISTIBLE* ATTRACTION TOWARDS THE *TOLERATED* GUEST.

HER BROTHER, WHO LOVED HER *TENDERLY*, WAS *APPALLED* AT THIS FANTASTIC PREFERENCE. LEAVING ASIDE THE *DEGRADATION* OF AN ALLIANCE WITH A *NAMELESS* MAN, AND THE POSSIBLE FACT THAT *HIS* PROPERTY, IN *DEFAULT* OF HEIRS *MALE*, MIGHT *PASS* INTO SUCH A ONE'S POWER...

...HE HAD *SENSE* TO COMPREHEND HEATHCLIFF'S *DISPOSITION*: TO KNOW THAT, THOUGH HIS *EXTERIOR* WAS ALTERED, HIS *MIND* WAS UNCHANGEABLE, AND *UNCHANGED*. AND HE *DREADED* THAT MIND: IT REVOLTED HIM: HE SHRANK FOREBODINGLY FROM THE IDEA OF COMMITTING *ISABELLA* TO ITS *KEEPING*. HE LAID THE *BLAME* ON HEATHCLIFF'S *DELIBERATE DESIGNING*.

WE HAD ALL REMARKED, DURING SOME TIME, THAT MISS LINTON *FRETTED* AND *PINED* OVER SOMETHING. SHE GREW *CROSS* AND *WEARISOME;* SNAPPING AND *TEASING* CATHERINE CONTINUALLY, AT THE IMMINENT RISK OF *EXHAUSTING* HER LIMITED *PATIENCE.*

IT IS **YOUR** HARSHNESS WHICH MAKES ME UNHAPPY.

HOW CAN YOU SAY I AM **HARSH**, YOU NAUGHTY FONDLING? YOU ARE SURELY LOSING YOUR **REASON.**

WHEN HAVE I BEEN **HARSH**, TELL ME?

YESTERDAY! IN OUR WALK ALONG THE MOOR: YOU TOLD ME TO RAMBLE WHERE I PLEASED, WHILE **YOU** SAUNTERED ON WITH **MR. HEATHCLIFF!**

AND **THAT'S** YOUR NOTION OF HARSHNESS?

YOU WISHED ME **AWAY**, BECAUSE YOU **KNOW** I WANTED TO BE WITH --

-- WITH **HIM.**

IT IS IMPOSSIBLE THAT YOU CAN COVET THE **ADMIRATION** OF HEATHCLIFF -- THAT YOU CONSIDER HIM AN **AGREEABLE** PERSON!

I HOPE I HAVE **MISUNDERSTOOD** YOU, ISABELLA?

NO, YOU HAVE **NOT.** I LOVE HIM **MORE** THAN EVER **YOU** LOVED EDGAR; AND **HE** MIGHT LOVE **ME**, IF **YOU** WOULD **LET** HIM!

I WOULDN'T BE YOU FOR A **KINGDOM**, THEN!

NELLY, HELP ME TO **CONVINCE** HER OF HER **MADNESS.**

TELL HER **WHAT** HEATHCLIFF IS: AN **UNRECLAIMED** CREATURE, WITHOUT REFINEMENT, WITHOUT CULTIVATION: AN ARID **WILDERNESS** OF FURZE AND WHINSTONE.

BANISH HIM FROM YOUR **THOUGHTS**, MISS. HE'S A BIRD OF **BAD** OMEN: NO MATE FOR YOU.

MRS. LINTON SPOKE **STRONGLY**, AND YET I **CAN'T** CONTRADICT HER. SHE **NEVER** WOULD REPRESENT HIM AS **WORSE** THAN HE IS.

MR. HEATHCLIFF IS **NOT** A FIEND: HE HAS AN **HONOURABLE** SOUL, AND A **TRUE** ONE!

THE DAY AFTER, THERE WAS A JUSTICE-MEETING AT THE NEXT TOWN; MY *MASTER* WAS OBLIGED TO ATTEND; AND MR. HEATHCLIFF, *AWARE* OF HIS *ABSENCE*, CALLED RATHER *EARLIER* THAN USUAL.

HEATHCLIFF, I'M PROUD TO SHOW YOU, AT **LAST**, SOMEBODY THAT **DOTES** ON YOU MORE THAN **MYSELF**. I EXPECT YOU TO FEEL **FLATTERED**.

MY POOR LITTLE SISTER-IN-LAW IS BREAKING HER **HEART** BY MERE **CONTEMPLATION** OF YOUR PHYSICAL AND MORAL **BEAUTY**. IT LIES IN YOUR **OWN** POWER TO BE EDGAR'S **BROTHER!**

NO, **NO**, ISABELLA, YOU **SHA'N'T** RUN OFF.

CATHERINE! I'D THANK YOU TO ADHERE TO THE **TRUTH** AND NOT SLANDER ME, EVEN IN JOKE!

MR. HEATHCLIFF, BE KIND ENOUGH TO BID THIS **FRIEND** OF YOURS **RELEASE** ME:

SHE **FORGETS** THAT YOU AND I ARE **NOT** INTIMATE ACQUAINTANCES; AND WHAT **AMUSES** HER IS **PAINFUL** TO ME BEYOND EXPRESSION.

AAH!

SCRATCH

THERE'S A **TIGRESS** INDEED! **BEGONE**, FOR GOD'S SAKE, AND **HIDE** YOUR **VIXEN** FACE! HOW **FOOLISH** TO REVEAL THOSE **TALONS** TO HIM. CAN'T YOU FANCY THE **CONCLUSIONS** HE'LL DRAW?

LOOK, HEATHCLIFF! THEY ARE INSTRUMENTS THAT WILL DO **EXECUTION** – YOU MUST BEWARE OF YOUR **EYES**.

I'D WRENCH THEM **OFF** HER FINGERS, IF THEY EVER MENACED **ME**.

SHE'S HER BROTHER'S **HEIR**, IS SHE NOT?

I SHOULD BE **SORRY** TO THINK SO. **ABSTRACT** YOUR MIND FROM THE SUBJECT AT PRESENT:

YOU ARE TOO **PRONE** TO COVET YOUR **NEIGHBOUR'S** GOODS; REMEMBER **THIS** NEIGHBOUR'S GOODS ARE **MINE**.

FROM THEIR TONGUES THEY *DID* DISMISS IT; AND CATHERINE, PROBABLY, FROM HER *THOUGHTS*. THE OTHER, I FELT *CERTAIN*, RECALLED IT *OFTEN* IN THE COURSE OF THE EVENING.

CHAPTER XI

THE *NEXT* TIME HEATHCLIFF CAME, MY YOUNG *LADY* CHANCED TO BE FEEDING SOME PIGEONS IN THE COURT.

SHE HAD NEVER SPOKEN A *WORD* TO HER SISTER-IN-LAW FOR *THREE DAYS;* BUT SHE HAD LIKEWISE DROPPED HER FRETFUL *COMPLAINING,* AND WE FOUND IT A GREAT *COMFORT.*

HEATHCLIFF HAD NOT THE HABIT OF BESTOWING A SINGLE UNNECESSARY *CIVILITY* ON MISS LINTON, I KNEW. NOW, AS *SOON* AS HE BEHELD HER, HIS *FIRST* PRECAUTION WAS TO TAKE A SWEEPING *SURVEY* OF THE HOUSE-FRONT. I WAS STANDING BY THE KITCHEN-WINDOW, BUT I DREW OUT OF *SIGHT.* SUPPOSING HIMSELF *UNSEEN*...

...THE SCOUNDREL HAD THE IMPUDENCE TO *EMBRACE* HER.

MRRRMMM!

JUDAS! TRAITOR! YOU ARE A HYPOCRITE, TOO, ARE YOU? A DELIBERATE DECEIVER.

WHO IS, NELLY?

YOUR WORTHLESS *FRIEND!* THE SNEAKING *RASCAL,* YONDER. I WONDER WILL HE HAVE THE *ART* TO FIND A PLAUSIBLE *EXCUSE* FOR MAKING *LOVE* TO MISS?

I COULDN'T WITHHOLD GIVING SOME *LOOSE* TO MY *INDIGNATION;* BUT CATHERINE ANGRILY INSISTED ON *SILENCE,* AND THREATENED TO *ORDER ME* OUT OF THE KITCHEN, IF I DARED TO BE SO *PRESUMPTUOUS* AS TO PUT IN MY *INSOLENT* TONGUE.

TO *HEAR* YOU, PEOPLE MIGHT THINK *YOU* WERE THE MISTRESS!

I HAVE A *RIGHT* TO KISS ISABELLA, IF SHE *CHOOSES;* AND YOU HAVE *NO RIGHT* TO OBJECT.

I AM NOT YOUR *HUSBAND:* YOU NEEDN'T BE JEALOUS OF *ME!*

I'M NOT JEALOUS *OF* YOU, I'M JEALOUS *FOR* YOU. IF YOU LIKE ISABELLA, YOU SHALL *MARRY* HER. BUT *DO* YOU LIKE HER? TELL THE *TRUTH,* HEATHCLIFF!

THERE, YOU *WON'T* ANSWER. I'M *CERTAIN* YOU DON'T.

AND WOULD MR. LINTON APPROVE OF HIS SISTER MARRYING *THAT MAN?*

MR. LINTON *SHOULD* APPROVE.

I COULD DO AS WELL *WITHOUT* HIS APPROBATION. AND AS TO *YOU,* CATHERINE, I WANT YOU TO BE *AWARE* THAT I KNOW YOU HAVE TREATED ME INFERNALLY – *INFERNALLY!*

AND IF YOU *FLATTER* YOURSELF THAT I DON'T *PERCEIVE* IT, YOU ARE A *FOOL;* AND IF YOU THINK I CAN BE *CONSOLED* BY SWEET WORDS, YOU ARE AN IDIOT:

AND IF YOU FANCY I'LL SUFFER *UNREVENGED,* I'LL CONVINCE YOU OF THE *CONTRARY,* IN A *VERY* LITTLE WHILE!

MEANTIME, *THANK* YOU FOR TELLING ME YOUR SISTER-IN-LAW'S SECRET: I *SWEAR* I'LL MAKE THE *MOST* OF IT. AND STAND YOU ASIDE!

WHAT *NEW* PHASE OF HIS CHARACTER IS *THIS?* I'VE TREATED YOU *INFERNALLY* – AND YOU'LL TAKE *REVENGE!*

HOW WILL YOU TAKE IT, *UNGRATEFUL BRUTE? HOW* HAVE I TREATED YOU *INFERNALLY?*

67

I SEEK **NO** REVENGE ON YOU. THAT'S NOT THE **PLAN**. THE **TYRANT** GRINDS DOWN HIS **SLAVES** AND THEY DON'T TURN AGAINST **HIM**; THEY CRUSH THOSE **BENEATH** THEM.

YOU ARE **WELCOME** TO TORTURE ME TO DEATH FOR YOUR **AMUSEMENT**, ONLY ALLOW ME TO AMUSE **MYSELF** A LITTLE IN THE **SAME** STYLE, AND **REFRAIN** FROM INSULT AS MUCH AS YOU ARE **ABLE**.

HAVING LEVELLED MY **PALACE**, DON'T ERECT A **HOVEL** AND COMPLACENTLY ADMIRE YOUR OWN **CHARITY** IN GIVING ME **THAT** FOR A HOME.

IF I IMAGINED YOU **REALLY** WISHED ME TO MARRY ISABELLA, I'D **CUT** MY **THROAT**!

HOW IS **THIS**? WHAT NOTION OF **PROPRIETY** MUST YOU HAVE TO **REMAIN** HERE, AFTER THE **LANGUAGE** WHICH HAS BEEN HELD TO YOU BY **THAT BLACKGUARD**?

I HAVE BEEN SO FAR **FORBEARING** WITH YOU, SIR; NOT THAT I WAS **IGNORANT** OF YOUR MISERABLE, DEGRADED CHARACTER, BUT I FELT YOU WERE ONLY **PARTLY** RESPONSIBLE FOR THAT; AND CATHERINE WISHING TO KEEP UP YOUR **ACQUAINTANCE**, I ACQUIESCED – **FOOLISHLY**.

YOUR PRESENCE IS A MORAL **POISON** THAT WOULD CONTAMINATE THE MOST **VIRTUOUS**: FOR THAT CAUSE, AND TO PREVENT **WORSE** CONSEQUENCES, I SHALL DENY YOU HEREAFTER **ADMISSION** INTO THIS HOUSE, AND GIVE NOTICE NOW THAT I REQUIRE YOUR **INSTANT DEPARTURE**.

THREE **MINUTES'** DELAY WILL RENDER IT **INVOLUNTARY** AND **IGNOMINIOUS**.

CATHY, THIS **LAMB** OF YOURS THREATENS LIKE A **BULL**! IT IS IN **DANGER** OF SPLITTING ITS **SKULL** AGAINST MY **KNUCKLES**.

BY GOD! MR. LINTON, I'M **MORTALLY** SORRY THAT YOU ARE NOT **WORTH** KNOCKING DOWN!

MRS. LINTON *SLAMMED* THE DOOR TO, AND *LOCKED* IT.

IF YOU HAVE NOT COURAGE TO *ATTACK* HIM, MAKE AN *APOLOGY*, OR ALLOW YOURSELF TO BE *BEATEN*.

IT WILL *CORRECT* YOU OF FEIGNING MORE *VALOUR* THAN YOU POSSESS.

HE TRIED TO *WREST* THE KEY FROM CATHERINE'S GRASP...

NO, I'LL *SWALLOW* THE KEY BEFORE *YOU* SHALL GET IT!

...AND FOR SAFETY, SHE *FLUNG* IT INTO THE HOTTEST PART OF THE FIRE.

MR. EDGAR WAS TAKEN WITH A NERVOUS *TREMBLING*.

OH, HEAVENS! IN OLD DAYS THIS WOULD WIN YOU *KNIGHTHOOD!*

WE ARE *VANQUISHED!* WE ARE *VANQUISHED!*

HEATHCLIFF WOULD AS SOON LIFT A FINGER AT *YOU* AS THE KING WOULD MARCH HIS *ARMY* AGAINST A COLONY OF *MICE*.

CHEER UP! YOU *SHA'N'T* BE *HURT!* YOUR TYPE IS *NOT* A LAMB, IT'S A SUCKING *LEVERET*.

I WISH YOU *JOY* OF THE MILK-BLOODED *COWARD*, CATHY! I COMPLIMENT YOU ON YOUR TASTE. AND *THAT* IS THE SLAVERING, SHIVERING THING YOU *PREFERRED* TO ME!

IS HE *WEEPING*, OR IS HE GOING TO *FAINT* FOR FEAR?

THWAK

AGHK!

WHILE HE *CHOKED*, MR. LINTON WALKED OUT.

THERE! YOU'VE *DONE* WITH COMING HERE.

GET *AWAY*, NOW; HE'LL RETURN WITH A BRACE OF *PISTOLS*, AND HALF-A-DOZEN *ASSISTANTS*. YOU'VE PLAYED ME AN ILL TURN, HEATHCLIFF!

DO YOU SUPPOSE I'M *GOING* WITH THAT BLOW BURNING IN MY *GULLET*?

BY HELL, *NO*! I'LL CRUSH HIS *RIBS* IN LIKE A ROTTEN *HAZEL-NUT* BEFORE I CROSS THE THRESHOLD!

IF I DON'T FLOOR HIM *NOW*, I SHALL *MURDER* HIM SOME TIME; SO, AS YOU *VALUE* HIS EXISTENCE, *LET ME GET AT HIM!*

HE IS NOT *COMING*. THERE'S THE *COACHMAN*, AND THE TWO GARDENERS; YOU'LL *SURELY* NOT WAIT TO BE THRUST INTO THE *ROAD* BY *THEM*!

EACH HAS A *BLUDGEON*; AND MASTER WILL BE *WATCHING* TO SEE THAT THEY *FULFIL* HIS ORDERS.

HEATHCLIFF SEIZED THE *POKER*, *SMASHED* THE LOCK FROM THE INNER DOOR, AND MADE HIS *ESCAPE* AS THEY TRAMPED IN.

REMAIN WHERE YOU *ARE*, CATHERINE. I WISH TO LEARN WHETHER YOU WILL *GIVE UP* HEATHCLIFF HEREAFTER, OR WILL YOU GIVE UP *ME*?

IT IS *IMPOSSIBLE* FOR YOU TO BE *MY* FRIEND AND *HIS* AT THE SAME TIME; AND I *ABSOLUTELY* REQUIRE TO KNOW WHICH YOU *CHOOSE*.

OH, FOR *MERCY'S* SAKE, LET US HEAR *NO MORE* OF IT NOW!

YOUR *COLD* BLOOD *CANNOT* BE WORKED INTO A FEVER: YOUR VEINS ARE FULL OF *ICE-WATER*; BUT MINE ARE BOILING, AND THE SIGHT OF SUCH *CHILLNESS* MAKES THEM DANCE.

I REQUIRE TO BE LET *ALONE!* I *DEMAND* IT! EDGAR, YOU – YOU *LEAVE* ME!

SHE RUSHED FROM THE ROOM TO HER CHAMBER, AND *SECURED* HER DOOR.

CHAPTER XII

MRS. LINTON ON THE THIRD DAY, *UNBARRED* HER DOOR, AND HAVING *FINISHED* THE *WATER* IN HER PITCHER AND DECANTER, DESIRED A *RENEWED* SUPPLY, AND A BASIN OF *GRUEL*, FOR SHE BELIEVED SHE WAS *DYING*.

HOW **LONG** IS IT SINCE I **SHUT** MYSELF IN HERE?

IT WAS **MONDAY** EVENING, AND **THIS** IS THURSDAY **NIGHT**, OR RATHER **FRIDAY** MORNING, AT PRESENT.

WHAT! OF THE SAME **WEEK?** ONLY THAT **BRIEF** TIME?

LONG ENOUGH TO LIVE ON **NOTHING** BUT COLD WATER AND **ILL-TEMPER**.

OH, I WILL **DIE**, SINCE NO ONE CARES **ANYTHING** ABOUT ME. WHAT IS THAT APATHETIC BEING **DOING?** HAS HE FALLEN INTO A **LETHARGY**, OR IS HE **DEAD?**

NEITHER, IF YOU MEAN MR. **LINTON**. HE'S **TOLERABLY** WELL, I THINK, THOUGH HIS **STUDIES** OCCUPY HIM RATHER **MORE** THAN THEY **OUGHT**:

HE IS CONTINUALLY AMONG HIS **BOOKS**, SINCE HE HAS NO **OTHER** SOCIETY.

AMONG HIS **BOOKS!** AND I **DYING!** I ON THE BRINK OF THE GRAVE!

MY **GOD!** DOES HE **KNOW** HOW I'M ALTERED?

WHY, MA'AM, THE MASTER HAS NO **IDEA** OF YOUR BEING **DERANGED**; AND OF COURSE HE DOES NOT **FEAR** THAT YOU WILL **LET** YOURSELF DIE OF **HUNGER**.

IF I WERE ONLY **SURE** IT WOULD KILL **HIM**, I'D KILL MYSELF **DIRECTLY!**

THESE THREE **AWFUL** NIGHTS, I'VE NEVER **CLOSED** MY LIDS – AND OH, I'VE BEEN **TORMENTED!** I'VE BEEN **HAUNTED**, NELLY!

BUT I BEGIN TO FANCY **YOU** DON'T **LIKE** ME. HOW **STRANGE!**

I THOUGHT, THOUGH EVERYBODY HATED AND **DESPISED** EACH **OTHER**, THEY COULD NOT **AVOID** LOVING ME.

AND THEY HAVE ALL TURNED TO **ENEMIES** IN A FEW HOURS: THEY HAVE, I'M **POSITIVE**; THE PEOPLE HERE.

SHE COULD NOT **BEAR** THE NOTION OF MR. LINTON'S PHILOSOPHICAL **RESIGNATION**. TOSSING ABOUT, SHE **TORE** THE PILLOW WITH HER **TEETH**. A MINUTE LATER, SHE WAS RANGING THE FEATHERS ACCORDING TO THEIR **SPECIES**.

THAT'S A **TURKEY'S**; AND THIS IS A WILD **DUCK'S**; AND THIS IS A **PIGEON'S**.

AH, THEY PUT **PIGEONS'** FEATHERS IN THE PILLOWS – NO **WONDER** I COULDN'T DIE!

THERE ARE TWO **CANDLES** ON THE TABLE MAKING THE BLACK PRESS **SHINE** LIKE JET.

THE **BLACK PRESS?** WHERE IS **THAT?** THERE'S NO PRESS IN THE ROOM, AND NEVER **WAS**.

IT'S AGAINST THE **WALL**, AS IT **ALWAYS** IS. IT DOES APPEAR **ODD** – I SEE A **FACE** IN IT!

DON'T YOU **SEE** THAT **FACE?**

AND SAY WHAT I **COULD**, I WAS INCAPABLE OF MAKING HER **COMPREHEND** IT TO BE HER **OWN**; SO I ROSE AND **COVERED** IT WITH A SHAWL.

IT'S **BEHIND** THERE **STILL!** AND IT STIRRED. WHO IS IT?

I HOPE IT WILL NOT COME **OUT** WHEN YOU ARE **GONE!**

OH! NELLY, THE ROOM IS **HAUNTED!** I'M AFRAID OF BEING **ALONE!**

A SOUND SLEEP WOULD DO YOU **GOOD**, MA'AM.

OH, IF I WERE BUT IN MY **OWN** BED IN THE **OLD** HOUSE!

BOTH THE **EXPRESSIONS** FLITTING OVER HER FACE, AND THE CHANGES OF HER **MOODS**, BEGAN TO **ALARM** ME TERRIBLY; AND BROUGHT TO MY RECOLLECTION HER **FORMER** ILLNESS, AND THE DOCTOR'S INJUNCTION THAT SHE SHOULD **NOT** BE CROSSED.

OH, SIR! MY POOR MISTRESS IS ILL.

CATHERINE ILL?

SHE HAS BEEN **FRETTING** HERE, AND EATING SCARCELY **ANYTHING**; BUT IT IS **NOTHING**.

IT IS **NOTHING**, IS IT, ELLEN DEAN? YOU SHALL ACCOUNT MORE **CLEARLY** FOR KEEPING ME **IGNORANT** OF THIS!

MONTHS OF SICKNESS COULD NOT CAUSE SUCH A **CHANGE**!

AH! YOU ARE **COME**, ARE YOU, EDGAR LINTON?

YOU ARE ONE OF **THOSE** THINGS THAT ARE **EVER** FOUND WHEN **LEAST** WANTED, AND WHEN YOU **ARE** WANTED, **NEVER**!

AM I **NOTHING** TO YOU ANY MORE?

DO YOU **LOVE** THAT WRETCH HEATH--

HUSH! I **DON'T** WANT YOU, EDGAR: I'M **PAST** WANTING YOU.

RETURN TO YOUR BOOKS. I'M GLAD YOU POSSESS A **CONSOLATION**, FOR ALL YOU HAD IN ME IS **GONE**.

HER MIND **WANDERS**, SIR. LET HER HAVE **QUIET**, AND PROPER ATTENDANCE, AND SHE'LL **RALLY**.

I DESIRE NO **FURTHER** ADVICE FROM **YOU**. THE NEXT TIME YOU BRING A **TALE** TO ME YOU SHALL **QUIT** MY SERVICE, ELLEN DEAN.

A **MANIAC'S** FURY KINDLED UNDER HER BROWS; SHE STRUGGLED **DESPERATELY** TO DISENGAGE HERSELF FROM LINTON'S ARMS. I FELT **NO** INCLINATION TO TARRY THE EVENT; AND, RESOLVING TO SEEK **MEDICAL AID** ON MY **OWN** RESPONSIBILITY, I QUITTED THE CHAMBER.

AH! NELLY HAS PLAYED TRAITOR.

LET ME **GO**, AND I'LL MAKE HER **RUE**! I'LL MAKE HER **HOWL** A RECANTATION!

MR. KENNETH, THE DOCTOR, ADVISED TO PRESERVE AROUND MRS. LINTON PERFECT AND CONSTANT *TRANQUILLITY*. NEXT MORNING, THE SERVANTS MOVED THROUGH THE HOUSE WITH *STEALTHY* TREAD. EVERY ONE WAS ACTIVE, BUT MISS ISABELLA.

OH, DEAR, **DEAR!** WHAT MUN WE HAVE **NEXT?**

MASTER, MASTER, OUR YOUNG LADY –

SPEAK **LOWER**, MARY. WHAT **AILS** YOUR YOUNG LADY?

SHE'S GONE, SHE'S **GONE!**

YON' HEATHCLIFF'S **RUN OFF** WI' HER!

THAT IS NOT **TRUE!** IT **CANNOT** BE: HOW HAS THE IDEA ENTERED YOUR **HEAD?**

ELLEN DEAN, GO AND **SEEK** HER.

I MET ON THE ROAD A **LAD** THAT FETCHES MILK HERE. HE **SAW** THEM TWO MILES OUT OF **GIMMERTON** NOT LONG AFTER **MIDNIGHT**.

I RAN AND PEEPED, FOR *FORM'S* SAKE, INTO ISABELLA'S *ROOM*; *CONFIRMING*, WHEN I RETURNED, THE SERVANT'S STATEMENT.

ARE WE TRYING ANY **MEASURES** FOR **OVERTAKING** AND BRINGING HER **BACK?**

HOW SHOULD WE **DO?**

SHE WENT OF HER **OWN** ACCORD; SHE HAD A **RIGHT** TO GO IF SHE PLEASED.

TROUBLE ME NO **MORE** ABOUT HER.

HEREAFTER SHE IS ONLY MY **SISTER** IN **NAME**: NOT BECAUSE I **DISOWN** HER, BUT BECAUSE **SHE** HAS DISOWNED **ME**.

AND THAT WAS **ALL** HE SAID ON THE SUBJECT, EXCEPT DIRECTING ME TO SEND WHAT *PROPERTY* SHE HAD IN THE HOUSE TO HER FRESH HOME, *WHEREVER* IT WAS, WHEN I KNEW IT.

FOR **TWO MONTHS** THE FUGITIVES REMAINED **ABSENT;** IN THOSE TWO MONTHS, MRS. LINTON ENCOUNTERED AND **CONQUERED** THE WORST **SHOCK** OF WHAT WAS DENOMINATED A **BRAIN FEVER.** NO **MOTHER** COULD HAVE NURSED AN ONLY **CHILD** MORE **DEVOTEDLY** THAN EDGAR TENDED **HER.**

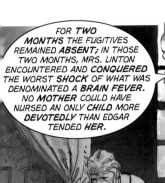

AND THERE WAS **DOUBLE** CAUSE TO DESIRE HER **RECOVERY,** FOR ON HER EXISTENCE DEPENDED THAT OF **ANOTHER:** WE CHERISHED THE **HOPE** THAT IN A LITTLE WHILE, MR. LINTON'S HEART WOULD BE **GLADDENED,** AND HIS LANDS SECURED FROM A STRANGER'S GRIPE, BY THE **BIRTH** OF AN **HEIR.**

ISABELLA SENT TO HER **BROTHER,** SOME SIX WEEKS FROM HER DEPARTURE, A SHORT NOTE, ANNOUNCING HER **MARRIAGE** WITH **HEATHCLIFF.** LINTON DID **NOT** REPLY.

HOUR AFTER HOUR HE WOULD SIT **BESIDE** HER, TRACING THE GRADUAL **RETURN** TO BODILY HEALTH, AND **FLATTERING** HIS TOO SANGUINE HOPES THAT SHE WOULD **SOON** BE ENTIRELY HER **FORMER** SELF.

CHAPTER XIII

IN A FORTNIGHT MORE, **I** GOT A LETTER WHICH I CONSIDERED **ODD,** COMING FROM THE PEN OF A **BRIDE** JUST OUT OF THE **HONEYMOON.**

DEAR ELLEN,

I came last night to Wuthering Heights, and heard that Catherine has been very ill. I must not write to her, I suppose, and my brother is either too angry or too distressed to answer what I sent him. I'd give the world to see his face again, and my heart is full of warm feelings for him, and Catherine!

I want to ask you two questions: the first is – How did you contrive to preserve the common sympathies of human nature when you resided here? I cannot recognise any sentiment which those around share with me.

The second question – Is Mr. Heathcliff mad? And if not, is he a devil? I beseech you to explain what I have married: that is, when you call to see me; and you must call, Ellen, very soon. Don't write, but come, and bring me something from Edgar.

I do hate Heathcliff – I am wretched – I have been a fool! Beware of uttering one breath of this to any one at the Grange. I shall expect you every day – don't disappoint me!

ISABELLA.

I WENT TO THE MASTER AND INFORMED HIM THAT HIS **SISTER** HAD ARRIVED AT THE **HEIGHTS,** AND SENT ME A LETTER EXPRESSING HER **SORROW** FOR MRS. LINTON'S SITUATION, AND HER ARDENT **DESIRE** TO **SEE** HIM; WITH A **WISH** THAT HE WOULD TRANSMIT TO HER SOME TOKEN OF **FORGIVENESS** BY ME.

FORGIVENESS! I HAVE **NOTHING** TO FORGIVE HER, ELLEN.

⟨ CHAPTER XIV ⟩

YOU MAY CALL AT WUTHERING HEIGHTS THIS **AFTERNOON,** IF YOU LIKE, AND SAY THAT I AM **NOT** ANGRY, BUT I'M **SORRY** TO HAVE **LOST** HER; ESPECIALLY AS I CAN **NEVER** THINK SHE'LL BE **HAPPY.**

IT IS OUT OF THE **QUESTION** MY GOING TO **SEE** HER, HOWEVER: WE ARE **ETERNALLY** DIVIDED; AND SHOULD SHE **REALLY** WISH TO **OBLIGE** ME, LET HER PERSUADE THE **VILLAIN** SHE HAS MARRIED TO **LEAVE** THE COUNTRY.

MY COMMUNICATION WITH **HEATHCLIFF'S** FAMILY SHALL **NOT** EXIST!

MR. EDGAR'S **COLDNESS** DEPRESSED ME **EXCEEDINGLY;** AND ALL THE WAY FROM THE GRANGE I **PUZZLED** MY BRAINS HOW TO PUT MORE **HEART** INTO WHAT HE SAID, WHEN I REPEATED IT.

I ENTERED WITHOUT KNOCKING. THERE NEVER WAS SUCH A DREARY, **DISMAL** SCENE AS THE FORMERLY **CHEERFUL** HOUSE PRESENTED!

I MUST CONFESS, THAT IF **I** HAD BEEN IN THE YOUNG LADY'S PLACE, I WOULD, AT LEAST, HAVE **SWEPT** THE HEARTH, AND **WIPED** THE TABLES WITH A **DUSTER.**

BUT SHE **ALREADY** PARTOOK OF THE PERVADING SPIRIT OF **NEGLECT** WHICH **ENCOMPASSED** HER.

HER PRETTY FACE WAS WAN AND *LISTLESS;* HER HAIR UNCURLED. PROBABLY SHE HAD NOT TOUCHED HER *DRESS* SINCE YESTER *EVENING.* SHE CAME FORWARD EAGERLY TO *GREET* ME;

AND HELD OUT ONE HAND TO TAKE THE EXPECTED *LETTER.* HEATHCLIFF *GUESSED* THE *MEANING* OF HER MANOEUVRES.

IF YOU HAVE GOT *ANYTHING* FOR ISABELLA, AS NO DOUBT YOU *HAVE,* NELLY, *GIVE* IT TO HER.

YOU NEEDN'T MAKE A *SECRET* OF IT: WE HAVE *NO* SECRETS BETWEEN US.

OH, I HAVE NOTHING.

MY MASTER BID ME *TELL* HIS SISTER THAT SHE MUST *NOT* EXPECT EITHER A *LETTER* OR A *VISIT* FROM HIM AT PRESENT.

HE SENDS HIS *LOVE,* MA'AM, AND HIS WISHES FOR YOUR *HAPPINESS,* BUT HE THINKS THAT AFTER THIS TIME, *HIS* HOUSEHOLD AND THE HOUSEHOLD HERE SHOULD *DROP* INTERCOMMUNICATION --

-- AS *NOTHING* COULD *COME* OF KEEPING IT UP.

MRS. LINTON IS NOW *JUST* RECOVERING. IF YOU *REALLY* HAVE A *REGARD* FOR HER, YOU'LL *SHUN* CROSSING HER WAY AGAIN:

NAY, YOU'LL MOVE *OUT* OF THIS COUNTRY *ENTIRELY.*

77

HAD **LINTON** BEEN IN MY PLACE, AND I IN **HIS**, THOUGH I **HATED** HIM WITH A HATRED THAT TURNED MY LIFE TO **GALL**, I NEVER WOULD HAVE RAISED A **HAND** AGAINST HIM AND BANISHED HIM FROM **HER** SOCIETY AS LONG AS **SHE** DESIRED **HIS.**

THE **MOMENT** HER REGARD CEASED, I WOULD HAVE **TORN** HIS **HEART** OUT, AND **DRANK** HIS **BLOOD!**

BUT, **TILL** THEN, I WOULD HAVE **DIED** BY INCHES BEFORE I **TOUCHED** A SINGLE **HAIR** OF HIS HEAD!

AND YET YOU HAVE **NO** SCRUPLES IN **COMPLETELY** RUINING ALL HOPES OF HER PERFECT **RESTORATION**, BY THRUSTING YOURSELF INTO HER REMEMBRANCE **NOW**, WHEN SHE HAS NEARLY **FORGOTTEN** YOU, AND INVOLVING HER IN A **NEW** TUMULT OF DISCORD AND **DISTRESS.**

YOU **SUPPOSE** SHE HAS NEARLY **FORGOTTEN** ME? OH, NELLY! YOU **KNOW** SHE HAS **NOT!**

YOU KNOW AS WELL AS **I** DO, THAT FOR EVERY THOUGHT SHE SPENDS ON **LINTON**, SHE SPENDS A **THOUSAND** ON ME!

I **WON'T** HEAR MY BROTHER DEPRECIATED IN **SILENCE!**

TAKE **CARE**, ELLEN! DON'T PUT **FAITH** IN A SINGLE **WORD** HE SPEAKS. HE'S A LYING **FIEND!** A **MONSTER**, AND **NOT** A HUMAN BEING! I'VE BEEN TOLD I MIGHT **LEAVE** HIM BEFORE; AND I'VE MADE THE **ATTEMPT**, BUT I **DARE** NOT REPEAT IT!

WHATEVER HE MAY **PRETEND**, HE WISHES TO **PROVOKE** EDGAR TO DESPERATION: HE SAYS HE HAS **MARRIED** ME ON PURPOSE TO OBTAIN **POWER** OVER HIM; AND HE **SHA'N'T** OBTAIN IT – I'LL **DIE** FIRST!

THE **SINGLE** PLEASURE I CAN **IMAGINE**, IS TO **DIE**, OR TO SEE HIM **DEAD!**

THAT WILL **DO** FOR THE PRESENT! YOU'RE NOT **FIT** TO BE YOUR OWN **GUARDIAN**, ISABELLA, NOW;

AND **I,** BEING YOUR LEGAL **PROTECTOR**, MUST RETAIN YOU IN MY CUSTODY, HOWEVER **DISTASTEFUL** THE OBLIGATION MAY BE.

GO UP-STAIRS; I HAVE SOMETHING TO SAY TO ELLEN DEAN IN **PRIVATE.** UP-STAIRS, I **TELL** YOU!

COME NOW, NELLY: I MUST EITHER **PERSUADE** YOU OR **COMPEL** YOU TO **AID** ME IN FULFILLING MY DETERMINATION TO **SEE** CATHERINE WITHOUT **DELAY.**

I SWEAR THAT I MEDIATE NO **HARM;** I ONLY WISH TO **HEAR** FROM HERSELF WHY SHE HAS BEEN ILL. I'D **WARN** YOU WHEN I CAME, AND THEN YOU MIGHT LET ME IN **UNOBSERVED,** AS SOON AS SHE WAS **ALONE.**

I CANNOT, SIR.

IN THAT CASE, I'LL TAKE **MEASURES** TO **SECURE** YOU, WOMAN!

YOU SHALL NOT **LEAVE** WUTHERING HEIGHTS. **DECIDE!**

WELL, I **ARGUED** AND **COMPLAINED,** AND FLATLY **REFUSED** HIM FIFTY TIMES; BUT IN THE LONG RUN HE **FORCED** ME TO AN **AGREEMENT.**

I **ENGAGED** TO CARRY A **LETTER** FROM HIM TO MY **MISTRESS;** AND SHOULD SHE **CONSENT,** I PROMISED TO LET HIM HAVE INTELLIGENCE OF LINTON'S NEXT **ABSENCE** FROM HOME, WHEN HE MIGHT COME, AND GET **IN** AS HE WAS ABLE.

I WOULDN'T BE **THERE,** AND MY FELLOW SERVANTS SHOULD BE EQUALLY **OUT** OF THE WAY.

WAS IT **RIGHT** OR **WRONG?** I FEAR IT WAS **WRONG,** THOUGH **EXPEDIENT.** NOTWITHSTANDING, MY JOURNEY HOMEWARD WAS **SADDER** THAN MY JOURNEY THITHER.

I HAD MADE UP MY MIND *NOT* TO GIVE MRS. LINTON THE LETTER TILL MY MASTER *WENT* SOMEWHERE. THE FOURTH DAY WAS SUNDAY, AND I BROUGHT IT TO HER AFTER THE FAMILY WERE GONE TO *CHURCH*.

THERE'S A *LETTER* FOR YOU, MRS. LINTON.

CHAPTER XV

YOU MUST READ IT IMMEDIATELY, BECAUSE IT WANTS AN *ANSWER*.

SHE DREW HER HAND AWAY.

MUST I *READ* IT, MA'AM?

IT IS FROM MR. *HEATHCLIFF*. WELL, HE WISHES TO *SEE* YOU.

HE'S IN THE *GARDEN* BY THIS TIME, AND *IMPATIENT* TO KNOW WHAT *ANSWER* I SHALL BRING.

A STEP TRAVERSED THE HALL; THE *OPEN* HOUSE WAS TOO *TEMPTING* FOR HEATHCLIFF TO RESIST *WALKING IN*.

OH, CATHY!

OH, MY *LIFE*!

81

I SHALL **NOT** BE AT PEACE. I'M NOT WISHING YOU GREATER **TORMENT** THAN I HAVE, HEATHCLIFF.

I ONLY WISH US **NEVER** TO BE **PARTED**: AND SHOULD A WORD OF MINE **DISTRESS** YOU HEREAFTER, THINK I FEEL THE **SAME** DISTRESS **UNDERGROUND**, AND FOR MY OWN SAKE, **FORGIVE** ME!

YOU NEVER **HARMED** ME IN YOUR LIFE. WON'T YOU COME HERE AGAIN? DO!

HEATHCLIFF WENT TO THE **BACK** OF HER CHAIR, AND LEANT OVER, BUT NOT SO **FAR** AS TO LET HER SEE HIS **FACE**, WHICH WAS FULL OF **EMOTION**.

SHE BENT ROUND TO LOOK AT HIM; HE WOULD NOT **PERMIT** IT.

OH, YOU **SEE**, NELLY, HE WOULD NOT RELENT A **MOMENT** TO KEEP ME OUT OF THE **GRAVE**.

THAT IS HOW I'M LOVED! WELL, NEVER MIND. THAT IS NOT **MY** HEATHCLIFF. I SHALL LOVE **MINE** YET; AND TAKE **HIM** WITH ME: HE'S IN MY **SOUL**.

I'M **TIRED** OF BEING ENCLOSED HERE. I'M WEARYING TO **ESCAPE** INTO THAT GLORIOUS WORLD, AND TO BE ALWAYS **THERE**.

NELLY, YOU THINK YOU ARE BETTER AND MORE **FORTUNATE** THAN I; IN FULL HEALTH AND STRENGTH: YOU ARE **SORRY** FOR ME – VERY SOON THAT WILL BE **ALTERED**. I SHALL BE **SORRY** FOR YOU.

I SHALL BE INCOMPARABLY **BEYOND** AND **ABOVE** YOU **ALL**.

IN HER EAGERNESS SHE ROSE.

HIS EYES **WIDE**, AND **WET** AT LAST, FLASHED **FIERCELY** ON HER.

AN INSTANT THEY HELD **ASUNDER**, AND THEN **HOW** THEY MET I HARDLY SAW, BUT CATHERINE MADE A **SPRING**, AND **HE** CAUGHT HER.

THEY WERE **LOCKED** IN AN EMBRACE FROM WHICH I THOUGHT MY MISTRESS WOULD **NEVER** BE **RELEASED ALIVE**. IN FACT, TO MY EYES, SHE SEEMED DIRECTLY **INSENSIBLE**.

WHY DID YOU **DESPISE** ME? WHY DID YOU BETRAY YOUR **OWN** HEART? YOU **DESERVE** THIS. YOU HAVE KILLED **YOURSELF**.

LET ME ALONE. LET ME **ALONE**. ≷sob≷ IF I'VE DONE **WRONG**, I'M **DYING** FOR IT. ≷sob≷ IT IS **ENOUGH**!

FORGIVE ME!

I **FORGIVE** YOU. I LOVE MY **MURDERER** – BUT **YOURS**! HOW CAN I?

I GREW VERY UNCOMFORTABLE; FOR THE AFTERNOON WORE FAST AWAY.

SERVICE IS OVER. MASTER WILL BE HERE IN HALF AN HOUR.

I MUST GO, CATHY.

BUT, IF I LIVE, I'LL SEE YOU AGAIN BEFORE YOU ARE ASLEEP. I WON'T STRAY FIVE YARDS FROM YOUR WINDOW.

YOU MUST NOT GO! YOU SHALL NOT, I TELL YOU.

I MUST — LINTON WILL BE UP IMMEDIATELY.

NO! OH, DON'T, DON'T GO. IT IS THE LAST TIME! EDGAR WILL NOT HURT US. HEATHCLIFF, I SHALL DIE! I SHALL DIE!

DAMN THE FOOL! THERE HE IS.

ARE YOU GOING TO LISTEN TO HER RAVINGS? SHE DOES NOT KNOW WHAT SHE SAYS.

WILL YOU RUIN HER, BECAUSE SHE HAS NOT WIT TO HELP HERSELF? WE ARE ALL DONE FOR — MASTER, MISTRESS, AND SERVANT.

MR. LINTON HASTENED HIS STEP AT THE NOISE. HE WAS BLANCHED WITH ASTONISHMENT AND RAGE.

UNLESS YOU BE A FIEND, HELP HER FIRST — THEN YOU SHALL SPEAK TO ME!

WITH GREAT DIFFICULTY WE MANAGED TO RESTORE HER TO SENSATION.

I SHALL NOT REFUSE TO GO OUT OF DOORS.

BUT I SHALL STAY IN THE GARDEN.

HEATHCLIFF DELIVERED THE HOUSE OF HIS LUCKLESS PRESENCE.

84

ABOUT TWELVE O'CLOCK, THAT NIGHT, WAS BORN THE **CATHERINE** YOU SAW AT WUTHERING HEIGHTS: A PUNY, **SEVEN-MONTHS'** CHILD...

...AND TWO HOURS AFTER THE MOTHER **DIED**, HAVING NEVER RECOVERED **SUFFICIENT** CONSCIOUSNESS TO **MISS** HEATHCLIFF, OR **KNOW** EDGAR.

AN **UNWELCOMED** INFANT IT WAS, **POOR** THING! IT MIGHT HAVE WAILED OUT OF LIFE, AND NOBODY **CARED** A MORSEL, DURING THOSE FIRST HOURS OF EXISTENCE. WE **REDEEMED** THE NEGLECT AFTERWARDS; BUT ITS BEGINNING WAS AS **FRIENDLESS** AS ITS **END** IS LIKELY TO BE.

A-WAAAH!

≒SOB≒

I INSTINCTIVELY **ECHOED** THE WORDS SHE HAD UTTERED A FEW **HOURS** BEFORE:

Incomparably beyond and above us all! Whether still on earth or now in heaven, her spirit is at home with God!

85

I VENTURED SOON AFTER SUNRISE TO QUIT THE ROOM AND *STEAL OUT* TO THE PURE REFRESHING *AIR*.

THE SERVANTS THOUGHT ME GONE TO SHAKE OFF THE *DROWSINESS* OF MY PROTRACTED *WATCH*;

IN *REALITY*, MY CHIEF MOTIVE WAS SEEING MR. HEATHCLIFF. HE HAD BEEN STANDING A *LONG* TIME LEANT AGAINST AN OLD ASH TREE, FOR I SAW A PAIR OF *OUZELS* PASSING NEAR TO HIM, BUSY IN BUILDING THEIR *NEST*.

THEY FLEW OFF AT MY APPROACH.

SHE'S *DEAD!* I'VE NOT WAITED FOR YOU TO LEARN *THAT*.

PUT YOUR HANDKERCHIEF *AWAY* – DON'T SNIVEL BEFORE ME.

DAMN YOU ALL! SHE WANTS *NONE* OF YOUR TEARS!

I WAS WEEPING AS MUCH FOR *HIM* AS *HER*. WE DO SOMETIMES *PITY* CREATURES THAT HAVE *NONE* OF THE FEELING EITHER FOR *THEMSELVES* OR *OTHERS*.

YES, SHE'S *DEAD!* GONE TO *HEAVEN*, I HOPE; WHERE WE MAY, EVERY *ONE*, JOIN HER, IF WE TAKE *DUE* WARNING AND *LEAVE* OUR *EVIL* WAYS TO FOLLOW *GOOD!*

DID SHE TAKE DUE WARNING, THEN? DID SHE DIE LIKE A *SAINT*?

COME, GIVE ME A *TRUE* HISTORY OF THE EVENT.

POOR *WRETCH!* YOU HAVE A HEART AND NERVES THE *SAME* AS YOUR BROTHER MEN! WHY SHOULD YOU BE ANXIOUS TO *CONCEAL* THEM? YOUR *PRIDE* CANNOT *BLIND* GOD!

MRS. LINTON'S **FUNERAL** WAS APPOINTED TO TAKE PLACE ON THE FRIDAY FOLLOWING HER DECEASE; AND TILL THEN HER COFFIN REMAINED **UNCOVERED**, AND STREWN WITH **FLOWERS** IN THE DRAWING-ROOM.

LINTON SPENT HIS DAYS AND NIGHTS THERE, A SLEEPLESS **GUARDIAN**. AND – A CIRCUMSTANCE CONCEALED FROM ALL BUT **ME** – HEATHCLIFF SPENT **HIS** NIGHTS, AT LEAST, OUTSIDE, **EQUALLY** A STRANGER TO REPOSE.

ON THE TUESDAY, A LITTLE AFTER **DARK**, WHEN MY MASTER HAD BEEN **COMPELLED** TO RETIRE A COUPLE OF HOURS, I WENT AND **OPENED** ONE OF THE WINDOWS; TO GIVE HIM A CHANCE OF BESTOWING ON THE FADING IMAGE OF HIS IDOL ONE **FINAL** ADIEU.

HE DID NOT OMIT TO **AVAIL** HIMSELF OF THE OPPORTUNITY, CAUTIOUSLY AND BRIEFLY.

INDEED, I SHOULDN'T HAVE DISCOVERED THAT HE HAD BEEN THERE, **EXCEPT** FOR OBSERVING ON THE FLOOR A CURL OF LIGHT **HAIR**, FASTENED WITH A SILVER **THREAD**;

WHICH, ON **EXAMINATION**, I ASCERTAINED TO HAVE BEEN TAKEN FROM A **LOCKET** HUNG ROUND **CATHERINE'S** NECK.

HEATHCLIFF HAD **OPENED** THE TRINKET AND CAST **OUT** ITS CONTENTS, REPLACING THEM BY A **BLACK LOCK** OF HIS **OWN**.

I TWISTED THE TWO, AND ENCLOSED THEM TOGETHER.

CHAPTER XVII

THAT FRIDAY MADE THE **LAST** OF OUR **FINE** DAYS, FOR A MONTH.

IN THE EVENING, THE WEATHER **BROKE**; THE WIND SHIFTED FROM SOUTH TO NORTH-EAST, AND BROUGHT **RAIN** FIRST, AND THEN **SLEET** AND **SNOW**.

DREARY, AND CHILL, AND **DISMAL** THAT MORROW DID CREEP OVER.

MY MASTER KEPT HIS **ROOM**; I TOOK POSSESSION OF THE LONELY **PARLOUR**, CONVERTING IT INTO A **NURSERY**: AND THERE I WAS SITTING, WITH THE **CHILD** LAID ON MY KNEE...

...WHEN THE DOOR OPENED, AND SOME PERSON **ENTERED**, OUT OF BREATH AND **LAUGHING**! I **SUPPOSED** IT ONE OF THE **MAIDS**.

HAVE **DONE**! HOW **DARE** YOU SHOW YOUR GIDDINESS HERE?

WHAT WOULD **MR.** LINTON SAY IF HE **HEARD** YOU?

EXCUSE ME! BUT I KNOW EDGAR IS IN BED, AND I CANNOT **STOP** MYSELF.

I HAVE **RUN** THE WHOLE WAY FROM **WUTHERING HEIGHTS**!

THE *INTRUDER* WAS MRS. HEATHCLIFF.

OH, I'M *ACHING* ALL OVER! DON'T BE *ALARMED!*

THERE SHALL BE AN *EXPLANATION* AS SOON AS I CAN GIVE IT;

ONLY JUST HAVE THE *GOODNESS* TO STEP OUT AND ORDER THE *CARRIAGE* TO TAKE ME ON TO *GIMMERTON*, AND TELL A SERVANT TO SEEK UP A FEW *CLOTHES* IN MY *WARDROBE*.

MY *DEAR* YOUNG LADY, I'LL STIR *NOWHERE*, AND HEAR *NOTHING*, TILL YOU HAVE REMOVED *EVERY* ARTICLE OF YOUR CLOTHES, AND PUT ON *DRY* THINGS;

AND *CERTAINLY* YOU SHALL *NOT* GO TO GIMMERTON *TONIGHT*.

FLING

CERTAINLY I *SHALL*; WALKING *OR* RIDING. THE *BRUTE* BEAST! *THIS* IS THE *LAST* THING OF HIS I HAVE ABOUT ME.

GIVE ME THE *POKER* – I'LL *SMASH* IT!

AND THEN I'LL *BURN* IT!

NECESSITY COMPELLED ME TO SEEK *SHELTER* HERE.

AH, HE WAS IN SUCH A *FURY!* IF HE HAD *CAUGHT* ME!

IT'S A *PITY* EARNSHAW IS NOT HIS *MATCH* IN *STRENGTH*: I WOULDN'T HAVE RUN TILL I'D SEEN HIM ALL BUT *DEMOLISHED*, HAD HINDLEY BEEN *ABLE* TO DO IT!

CATHERINE HAD AN AWFULLY *PERVERTED* TASTE TO ESTEEM HIM SO *DEARLY*, KNOWING HIM SO WELL. *MONSTER!* WOULD THAT HE COULD BE *BLOTTED* OUT OF *CREATION*, AND OUT OF MY *MEMORY!*

HUSH, HUSH! HE'S A *HUMAN* BEING. BE MORE *CHARITABLE*: THERE ARE *WORSE* MEN THAN *HE* IS YET!

HE'S *NOT* A HUMAN BEING, AND HE HAS *NO* CLAIM ON MY CHARITY.

YESTER-EVENING I SAT IN MY NOOK READING SOME OLD BOOKS TILL *LATE* ON TOWARDS TWELVE. *HINDLEY* SAT WITH ME.

HEATHCLIFF WENT OUT ON HIS *WATCH.*

MY COMPANION SPOKE TO ME.

YOU, AND I, HAVE EACH A GREAT *DEBT* TO SETTLE WITH THE *MAN* OUT *YONDER!* IF WE WERE NEITHER OF US *COWARDS,* WE MIGHT COMBINE TO *DISCHARGE* IT.

ARE YOU AS *SOFT* AS YOUR *BROTHER?* ARE YOU WILLING TO *ENDURE* TO THE *LAST,* AND NOT ONCE ATTEMPT A *REPAYMENT?*

I'M WEARY OF ENDURING *NOW,* AND I'D BE GLAD OF A *RETALIATION* THAT WOULDN'T RECOIL ON *MYSELF;*

BUT *TREACHERY* AND *VIOLENCE* ARE SPEARS POINTED AT *BOTH* ENDS; THEY WOUND THOSE WHO *RESORT* TO THEM *WORSE* THAN THEIR ENEMIES.

TREACHERY AND VIOLENCE ARE A *JUST RETURN* FOR *TREACHERY* AND *VIOLENCE!*

MRS. HEATHCLIFF, I'LL ASK YOU TO DO *NOTHING;* BUT SIT STILL AND BE *DUMB.* TELL ME NOW, *CAN* YOU?

I'M SURE YOU WOULD HAVE AS MUCH *PLEASURE* AS I IN WITNESSING THE *CONCLUSION* OF THE FIEND'S *EXISTENCE;* HE'LL BE YOUR *DEATH* UNLESS YOU *OVERREACH* HIM; AND HE'LL BE MY RUIN.

DAMN THE *HELLISH VILLAIN!*

WE HEARD THE SOUND OF THE KITCHEN LATCH. HEATHCLIFF HAD *RETURNED* FROM HIS WATCH.

PROMISE TO **HOLD** YOUR TONGUE, AND BEFORE THAT CLOCK **STRIKES** – IT WANTS **THREE MINUTES** OF ONE – YOU'RE A **FREE WOMAN!**

I'LL **NOT** HOLD MY TONGUE. YOU **MUSTN'T** TOUCH HIM.

LET THE DOOR REMAIN **SHUT,** AND BE **QUIET!**

NO! I'VE FORMED MY **RESOLUTION,** AND BY **GOD** I'LL **EXECUTE** IT!

I'LL DO YOU A **KINDNESS** IN SPITE OF YOURSELF, AND HARETON **JUSTICE!**

I MIGHT AS WELL HAVE STRUGGLED WITH A *BEAR,* OR REASONED WITH A *LUNATIC.* THE ONLY RESOURCE LEFT ME WAS TO *WARN* HIS INTENDED *VICTIM.*

YOU'D BETTER SEEK SHELTER SOMEWHERE **ELSE** TO-NIGHT! MR. EARNSHAW HAS A MIND TO **SHOOT** YOU, IF YOU **PERSIST** IN ENDEAVOURING TO **ENTER.**

YOU'D **BETTER** OPEN THE DOOR, YOU –

I SHALL NOT **MEDDLE** IN THE MATTER. COME IN AND GET **SHOT,** IF YOU PLEASE. I'VE DONE MY **DUTY.**

EARNSHAW *SWORE* PASSIONATELY AT ME: AFFIRMING THAT I *LOVED* THE VILLAIN YET; AND CALLING ME ALL SORTS OF *NAMES* FOR THE *BASE* SPIRIT I EVINCED.

SMAAASH

ISABELLA, LET ME IN, OR I'LL *MAKE* YOU *REPENT!*

92

HE'S THERE, IS HE? IF I CAN GET MY ARM OUT I CAN HIT HIM!

HE FLUNG HIMSELF ON EARNSHAW'S WEAPON...

...AND WRENCHED IT FROM HIS GRASP.

BLAM

AARGGHHH!

HEATHCLIFF SPRUNG IN.

THE RUFFIAN KICKED AND TRAMPLED ON HIM...

THWAK

THWAK

...AND DASHED HIS HEAD REPEATEDLY ON THE FLAGS.

THUD THUD

OH, IF GOD WOULD BUT GIVE ME **STRENGTH** TO **STRANGLE** HIM IN MY LAST AGONY, I'D GO TO HELL WITH **JOY**.

GET UP, AND **BEGONE** OUT OF MY **SIGHT**! GET UP, WRETCHED IDIOT, BEFORE I STAMP YOU TO **DEATH**!

NAY, IT'S NOT **ENOUGH** THAT HE HAS MURDERED **ONE** OF YOU. **EVERY ONE** KNOWS YOUR SISTER WOULD HAVE BEEN **LIVING NOW** HAD IT **NOT** BEEN FOR MR. HEATHCLIFF.

IT IS PREFERABLE TO BE **HATED** THAN **LOVED** BY HIM. WHEN I RECOLLECT HOW **HAPPY** WE WERE – HOW HAPPY **CATHERINE** WAS BEFORE **HE** CAME – I'M FIT TO **CURSE** THE DAY.

IF POOR CATHERINE HAD **TRUSTED** YOU, AND ASSUMED THE RIDICULOUS, CONTEMPTIBLE, **DEGRADING** TITLE OF **MRS. HEATHCLIFF**, SHE WOULD SOON HAVE PRESENTED A **SIMILAR** PICTURE!

SHE WOULDN'T HAVE BORNE YOUR **ABOMINABLE** BEHAVIOUR QUIETLY: THE DETESTATION AND **DISGUST** MUST HAVE FOUND A **VOICE**.

YAAAH!

≈GASP≈

THUNK

BLEST AS A SOUL ESCAPED FROM **PURGATORY**, I BOUNDED, LEAPED, AND **FLEW** DOWN THE STEEP ROAD...

...AND FAR **RATHER** WOULD I BE CONDEMNED TO A **PERPETUAL** DWELLING IN THE INFERNAL REGIONS, THAN, EVEN FOR **ONE** NIGHT, ABIDE BENEATH THE ROOF OF **WUTHERING HEIGHTS** AGAIN.

ISABELLA WAS DRIVEN AWAY, **NEVER** TO REVISIT THIS NEIGHBOURHOOD: BUT A REGULAR **CORRESPONDENCE** WAS ESTABLISHED BETWEEN HER AND MY MASTER WHEN THINGS WERE MORE **SETTLED.**

I BELIEVE HER NEW ABODE WAS IN THE SOUTH, NEAR **LONDON;** THERE SHE HAD A **SON** BORN, A FEW MONTHS SUBSEQUENT TO HER **ESCAPE.**

HE WAS CHRISTENED **LINTON,** AND, FROM THE FIRST, SHE REPORTED HIM TO BE AN AILING, **PEEVISH** CREATURE.

MR. HEATHCLIFF, **MEETING** ME ONE DAY IN THE VILLAGE, INQUIRED **WHERE** SHE LIVED. I **REFUSED** TO TELL. THOUGH I WOULD GIVE NO INFORMATION, HE DISCOVERED, THROUGH SOME OF THE OTHER SERVANTS, **BOTH** HER PLACE OF RESIDENCE AND THE EXISTENCE OF THE **CHILD.** ON HEARING ITS **NAME,** HE OBSERVED:

THEY WISH ME TO HATE IT **TOO,** DO THEY?

I DON'T THINK THEY WISH YOU TO KNOW **ANY** THING ABOUT IT.

BUT I'LL **HAVE IT,** WHEN I **WANT** IT. THEY MAY RECKON ON THAT!

FORTUNATELY, ITS MOTHER DIED **BEFORE** THE TIME ARRIVED, SOME **THIRTEEN YEARS** AFTER THE DECEASE OF CATHERINE, WHEN LINTON WAS **TWELVE,** OR A LITTLE MORE.

95

MY MASTER WAS TOO **GOOD** TO BE THOROUGHLY UNHAPPY LONG. **HE** DIDN'T PRAY FOR CATHERINE'S SOUL TO **HAUNT HIM**. HE HAD **EARTHLY** CONSOLATION AND AFFECTIONS. HIS **COLDNESS** TOWARDS HIS **DAUGHTER** MELTED AS FAST AS SNOW IN APRIL, AND ERE THE TINY THING COULD STAMMER A WORD OR TOTTER A STEP, IT WIELDED A **DESPOT'S** SCEPTRE IN HIS HEART.

IT WAS NAMED **CATHERINE;** BUT HE NEVER CALLED IT THE NAME IN **FULL,** AS HE HAD NEVER CALLED THE **FIRST** CATHERINE SHORT: PROBABLY BECAUSE **HEATHCLIFF** HAD A HABIT OF DOING SO.

THE LITTLE ONE WAS ALWAYS **CATHY:** IT FORMED TO HIM A **DISTINCTION** FROM THE MOTHER, AND YET A **CONNECTION** WITH HER; AND HIS ATTACHMENT SPRANG FROM ITS **RELATION** TO HER, FAR MORE THAN FROM ITS BEING HIS **OWN.**

ONE MORNING, **MR. KENNETH,** THE **DOCTOR,** CAME RIDING INTO THE YARD.

WELL, NELLY, IT'S **YOURS** AND MY TURN TO GO INTO **MOURNING** AT PRESENT.

WHO'S GIVEN US THE SLIP **NOW,** DO YOU THINK?

NOT MR. **HEATHCLIFF,** SURELY?

WHAT! WOULD YOU HAVE **TEARS** FOR HIM?

NO, HEATHCLIFF'S A **TOUGH** YOUNG FELLOW: HE LOOKS **BLOOMING** TO-DAY. I'VE JUST **SEEN** HIM. HE'S RAPIDLY REGAINING **FLESH** SINCE HE LOST HIS **BETTER** HALF.

WHO **IS** IT, THEN, MR. KENNETH?

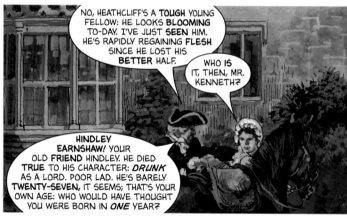

HINDLEY EARNSHAW! YOUR OLD **FRIEND** HINDLEY. HE DIED **TRUE** TO HIS CHARACTER: **DRUNK** AS A LORD. POOR LAD. HE'S BARELY **TWENTY-SEVEN,** IT SEEMS; THAT'S YOUR OWN AGE: WHO WOULD HAVE THOUGHT YOU WERE BORN IN **ONE** YEAR?

I COULD NOT HINDER MYSELF FROM PONDERING, "HAD HE **HAD** FAIR PLAY?" THE GUEST WAS NOW THE **MASTER** OF WUTHERING HEIGHTS:

HE HELD FIRM **POSSESSION,** AND PROVED TO THE ATTORNEY – WHO, IN HIS TURN, PROVED IT TO MR. LINTON – THAT EARNSHAW HAD **MORTGAGED** EVERY YARD OF LAND HE OWNED FOR **CASH** TO SUPPLY HIS MANIA FOR **GAMING;** AND HE, **HEATHCLIFF,** WAS THE **MORTGAGEE.**

IN THAT MANNER **HARETON,** WHO SHOULD NOW BE THE FIRST GENTLEMAN IN THE NEIGHBOURHOOD, WAS REDUCED TO A STATE OF COMPLETE **DEPENDENCE** ON HIS FATHER'S INVETERATE **ENEMY;** AND LIVES IN HIS **OWN** HOUSE AS A **SERVANT,** DEPRIVED OF THE ADVANTAGE OF WAGES: QUITE **UNABLE** TO **RIGHT** HIMSELF, BECAUSE OF HIS **FRIENDLESSNESS,** AND HIS **IGNORANCE** THAT HE HAS BEEN **WRONGED.**

THE TWELVE YEARS, *FOLLOWING* THAT *DISMAL* PERIOD, WERE THE *HAPPIEST* OF MY LIFE: MY GREATEST TROUBLES IN THEIR PASSAGE ROSE FROM OUR LITTLE LADY'S *TRIFLING* ILLNESSES, WHICH SHE HAD TO EXPERIENCE IN COMMON WITH *ALL* CHILDREN, RICH *AND* POOR.

CHAPTER XVIII

SHE WAS THE MOST *WINNING* THING THAT EVER BROUGHT *SUNSHINE* INTO A DESOLATE HOUSE: A *REAL* BEAUTY IN FACE, WITH THE *EARNSHAWS'* HANDSOME EYES, BUT THE *LINTONS'* FAIR SKIN AND SMALL FEATURES, AND YELLOW CURLING HAIR.

HER SPIRIT WAS *HIGH*, THOUGH NOT *ROUGH*, AND QUALIFIED BY A HEART SENSITIVE AND LIVELY TO *EXCESS* IN ITS AFFECTIONS.

HOWEVER, SHE HAD *FAULTS* TO FOIL HER GIFTS. A PROPENSITY TO BE *SAUCY* WAS ONE; AND A *PERVERSE WILL*, THAT INDULGED CHILDREN *INVARIABLY* ACQUIRE, WHETHER THEY BE *GOOD TEMPERED* OR *CROSS*.

IF A SERVANT CHANCED TO *VEX* HER, IT WAS ALWAYS:

I SHALL TELL *PAPA*!

AND IF HE *REPROVED* HER, YOU WOULD HAVE THOUGHT IT *HEARTBREAKING* BUSINESS: I DON'T THINK HE EVER *DID* SPEAK A *HARSH* WORD TO HER.

TILL SHE REACHED THE AGE OF *THIRTEEN*, SHE HAD NOT *ONCE* BEEN BEYOND THE RANGE OF THE PARK BY HERSELF. THEN, IN *JULY*, SHE TROTTED OFF ON HER *PONY*, AND THE NAUGHTY THING NEVER MADE HER APPEARANCE AT *TEA*.

THE ABRUPT DESCENT OF *PENISTONE CRAGS* PARTICULARLY ATTRACTED HER *NOTICE*: IT STRUCK ME DIRECTLY SHE MUST HAVE HEADED *THERE*.

THE CRAGS LIE ABOUT A MILE AND A HALF *BEYOND* MR. HEATHCLIFF'S PLACE, AND THAT IS *FOUR* FROM THE GRANGE, SO I BEGAN TO FEAR *NIGHT* WOULD FALL ERE I COULD *REACH* THEM.

I WALKED MILE AFTER MILE, TILL A TURN BROUGHT ME IN VIEW OF THE *HEIGHTS*.

A WOMAN WHOM *I KNEW* ANSWERED. I ENTERED, AND *BEHELD* MY STRAY LAMB, *PERFECTLY* AT *HOME*, LAUGHING AND CHATTERING TO HARETON – NOW A *STRONG* LAD OF *EIGHTEEN*.

VERY WELL, MISS.

I'LL NOT TRUST YOU OVER THE *THRESHOLD* AGAIN, YOU NAUGHTY, *NAUGHTY* GIRL!

AHA, ELLEN! YOU'VE *FOUND* ME OUT. HAVE YOU EVER BEEN *HERE* IN YOUR LIFE BEFORE?

I'M *DREADFULLY* GRIEVED AT YOU, MISS CATHY: YOU'VE DONE *EXTREMELY* WRONG!

IT'S NO USE *POUTING* AND *CRYING*: THAT WON'T REPAY THE *TROUBLE* I'VE HAD, SCOURING THE COUNTRY AFTER *YOU*.

WHAT HAVE I *DONE*? PAPA WILL NOT *SCOLD* ME, ELLEN – HE'S *NEVER* CROSS, LIKE YOU!

COME, COME! NOW, LET US HAVE NO *PETULANCE*. OH, FOR SHAME! YOU *THIRTEEN* YEARS OLD, AND *SUCH* A BABY!

IF YOU WERE AWARE *WHOSE* HOUSE THIS IS, YOU'D BE *GLAD* ENOUGH TO GET *OUT*.

IT'S YOUR *FATHER'S*, ISN'T IT?

NAY.

WHOSE THEN – YOUR MASTER'S? NOW, GET MY HORSE – MAKE HASTE!

I'LL SEE THEE DAMNED BEFORE I BE THY SERVANT!

YOU'LL SEE ME WHAT?

YOU BRING THE PONY!

SOFTLY, MISS. YOU'LL LOSE NOTHING BY BEING CIVIL. THOUGH MR. HARETON, THERE, BE NOT THE MASTER'S SON, HE'S YOUR COUSIN: AND I WAS NEVER HIRED TO SERVE YOU.

HE, MY COUSIN! HE'S NOT – HE'S NOT MY COUSIN, ELLEN! MY COUSIN IS IN LONDON: MY COUSIN IS A GENTLEMAN'S SON.

HUSH. HUSH! PEOPLE CAN HAVE MANY COUSINS, AND OF ALL SORTS, MISS CATHY, WITHOUT BEING ANY WORSE FOR IT.

THE LANGUAGE HE HAD HELD TO HER RANKLED IN HER HEART; SHE WHO WAS ALWAYS "LOVE," AND "DARLING," AND "QUEEN," AND "ANGEL," WITH EVERYBODY AT THE GRANGE, TO BE INSULTED SO SHOCKINGLY BY A STRANGER! SHE DID NOT COMPREHEND IT; AND HARD WORK I HAD TO OBTAIN A PROMISE THAT SHE WOULD NOT LAY THE GRIEVANCE BEFORE HER FATHER.

SHE PLEDGED HER WORD, AND KEPT IT FOR MY SAKE. AFTER ALL, SHE WAS A SWEET LITTLE GIRL.

I THOUGHT, IN HARETON, I COULD DETECT A MIND OWNING BETTER QUALITIES THAN HIS FATHER EVER POSSESSED. GOOD THINGS LOST AMID A WILDERNESS OF WEEDS, TO BE SURE; YET, NOTWITHSTANDING, EVIDENCE OF A WEALTHY SOIL, THAT MIGHT YIELD LUXURIANT CROPS UNDER OTHER AND FAVOURABLE CIRCUMSTANCES.

CHAPTER XIX

A *LETTER*, EDGED WITH BLACK, ANNOUNCED THAT ISABELLA WAS *DEAD.* THE MASTER BID ME ARRANGE A ROOM, AND OTHER ACCOMMODATIONS, FOR *LINTON,* HIS YOUTHFUL *NEPHEW.*

CATHERINE RAN WILD WITH *JOY* AT THE IDEA OF WELCOMING HER FATHER BACK; AND INDULGED MOST SANGUINE *ANTICIPATIONS* OF THE INNUMERABLE *EXCELLENCES* OF HER "*REAL*" COUSIN.

AH, I SEE SOME *DUST* ON THE ROAD – THEY ARE *COMING!*

WHILE SHE AND HER FATHER EXCHANGED CARESSES...

... *I* TOOK A PEEP IN TO SEE AFTER LINTON. A PALE, *DELICATE,* EFFEMINATE BOY, WHO MIGHT HAVE BEEN TAKEN FOR MY MASTER'S YOUNGER *BROTHER,* SO STRONG WAS THE *RESEMBLANCE:* BUT THERE WAS A SICKLY *PEEVISHNESS* IN HIS ASPECT THAT EDGAR LINTON *NEVER* HAD.

THIS IS YOUR COUSIN *CATHY,* LINTON. SHE'S FOND OF *YOU* ALREADY.

TRY TO BE *CHEERFUL* NOW; THE TRAVELLING IS AT AN *END,* AND YOU HAVE NOTHING TO DO BUT *REST* AND *AMUSE* YOURSELF AS YOU PLEASE.

LET ME GO TO *BED,* THEN.

OH, HE'LL DO VERY WELL. *VERY* WELL, IF WE CAN *KEEP* HIM, ELLEN. THE COMPANY OF A CHILD OF HIS *OWN* AGE WILL INSTIL *NEW* SPIRIT INTO HIM SOON, AND BY *WISHING* FOR STRENGTH HE'LL *GAIN* IT.

AYE, *IF* WE CAN *KEEP* HIM!

OUR *DOUBTS* WERE PRESENTLY DECIDED; EVEN *EARLIER* THAN I EXPECTED. I HAD JUST SEEN LINTON *ASLEEP*, WHEN A MAID STEPPED OUT OF THE KITCHEN AND INFORMED ME THAT MR. HEATHCLIFF'S SERVANT *JOSEPH* WAS AT THE DOOR, AND WISHED TO *SPEAK* WITH THE MASTER.

HEATHCLIFF HAS SEND ME FOR HIS *LAD*, UN AW *MUNN'T* GOA BACK *'BAHT* HIM.

TELL MR. HEATHCLIFF THAT HIS SON SHALL COME TO WUTHERING HEIGHTS *TO-MORROW*. HE IS IN BED, AND TOO *TIRED* TO GO THE DISTANCE NOW.

YOU MAY *ALSO* TELL HIM THAT THE *MOTHER* OF LINTON DESIRED HIM TO REMAIN UNDER *MY* GUARDIANSHIP; AND, AT PRESENT, HIS *HEALTH* IS VERY PRECARIOUS.

NOA! NOA! THAT MANES *NOWT* – HEATHCLIFF MAKS *NOA* 'CAHNT UH T' MOTHER, NUR *YAH* NORTHER;

BUD HE'LL *HEV* HIS LAD; UND AW MUN TAK' HIM – SOA NAH YAH *KNAW*!

YOU SHALL *NOT* TO-NIGHT! WALK OUT AT *ONCE*, AND *REPEAT* TO YOUR MASTER WHAT *I* HAVE SAID.

ELLEN, SHOW HIM OUT.

GO!

VARRAH *WEEL*! TUH MORN, HE'S COME *HISSELN*, AND THRUST HIM AHT, IF YAH *DARR*!

TO OBVIATE THE DANGER OF THIS *THREAT* BEING FULFILLED, MR. LINTON COMMISSIONED ME TO TAKE THE BOY HOME *EARLY*, ON CATHERINE'S *PONY*.

CHAPTER XX

LINTON WAS VERY *RELUCTANT* TO BE ROUSED FROM HIS BED AT FIVE O'CLOCK, AND *ASTONISHED* TO BE INFORMED THAT HE MUST PREPARE FOR *FURTHER* TRAVELLING;

BUT I SOFTENED OFF THE MATTER BY STATING THAT HE WAS GOING TO SPEND SOME TIME WITH HIS *FATHER*, MR. HEATHCLIFF, WHO WISHED TO SEE HIM SO *MUCH*.

MY *FATHER*! MAMMY NEVER TOLD ME I HAD A FATHER. WHERE DOES HE *LIVE*?

HE LIVES A LITTLE *DISTANCE* FROM THE *GRANGE*.

I'D *RATHER* STAY WITH UNCLE.

YOU SHOULD BE *GLAD* TO GO HOME, AND *SEE* HIM. YOU MUST *TRY* TO LOVE HIM, AS YOU DID YOUR *MOTHER*, AND THEN *HE* WILL LOVE *YOU*.

WHY HAVE I NOT *HEARD* OF HIM *BEFORE*? WHY DIDN'T MAMMA AND HE LIVE *TOGETHER*, AS *OTHER* PEOPLE DO?

HE HAD *BUSINESS* TO KEEP HIM IN THE *NORTH*, AND YOUR MOTHER'S *HEALTH* REQUIRED HER TO *RESIDE* IN THE SOUTH.

WELL, WHAT IS MY FATHER *LIKE*? IS HE AS YOUNG AND HANDSOME AS *UNCLE*?

HE'S AS YOUNG, BUT HE HAS *BLACK* HAIR AND EYES, AND LOOKS *STERNER*; AND HE IS TALLER AND *BIGGER* ALTOGETHER.

HE'LL NOT SEEM TO YOU SO *GENTLE* AND *KIND* AT FIRST, PERHAPS, BECAUSE IT IS NOT HIS *WAY* –

STILL, MIND YOU, BE *FRANK* AND *CORDIAL* WITH HIM; AND NATURALLY HE'LL BE *FONDER* OF YOU THAN ANY UNCLE, FOR YOU ARE HIS *OWN*.

BLACK HAIR AND EYES! I CAN'T FANCY HIM. THEN I AM NOT *LIKE* HIM, AM I?

NOT *MUCH*.

NOT A MORSEL.

HALLO, NELLY! I FEARED I SHOULD HAVE TO COME DOWN AND *FETCH* MY PROPERTY *MYSELF*. YOU'VE *BROUGHT* IT, HAVE YOU?

LET US SEE WHAT WE CAN *MAKE* OF IT.

HEH-HEH! GOD! WHAT A BEAUTY! WHAT A LOVELY, CHARMING THING!

HAVEN'T THEY REARED IT ON SNAILS AND SOUR MILK, NELLY? OH, DAMN MY SOUL! BUT THAT'S WORSE THAN I EXPECTED – AND THE DEVIL KNOWS I WAS NOT SANGUINE!

THOU ART THY MOTHER'S CHILD, ENTIRELY! WHERE IS MY SHARE IN THEE, PULING CHICKEN? DO YOU KNOW ME?

NO.

I HOPE YOU'LL BE KIND TO THE BOY, MR. HEATHCLIFF, OR YOU'LL NOT KEEP HIM LONG;

AND HE'S ALL YOU HAVE AKIN IN THE WIDE WORLD, THAT YOU WILL EVER KNOW – REMEMBER.

I'LL BE VERY KIND TO HIM, YOU NEEDN'T FEAR.

HE'S MINE, AND I WANT THE TRIUMPH OF SEEING MY DESCENDANT FAIRLY LORD OF THEIR ESTATES. I DESPISE HIM FOR HIMSELF, AND HATE HIM FOR THE MEMORIES HE REVIVES!

I WISH I FOUND HIM A WORTHY OBJECT OF PRIDE, BUT I'M BITTERLY DISAPPOINTED WITH THE WHEY-FACED WHINING WRETCH!

HAVING NO EXCUSE FOR LINGERING LONGER, I SLIPPED OUT, WHILE LINTON WAS ENGAGED IN TIMIDLY REBUFFING THE ADVANCES OF A FRIENDLY SHEEP-DOG.

BUT THAT CONSIDERATION IS SUFFICIENT: HE'S AS SAFE WITH ME, AND SHALL BE TENDED AS CAREFULLY AS YOUR MASTER TENDS HIS OWN.

BUT HE WAS TOO MUCH ON THE ALERT TO BE CHEATED: AS I CLOSED THE DOOR, I HEARD A CRY, AND A FRANTIC REPETITION OF THE WORDS:

DON'T LEAVE ME! I'LL NOT STAY HERE! I'LL NOT STAY HERE!

CHAPTER XXI

WE HAD **SAD** WORK WITH LITTLE CATHY THAT DAY: SHE ROSE IN **HIGH** GLEE, EAGER TO **JOIN** HER COUSIN; AND SUCH **PASSIONATE** TEARS AND LAMENTATIONS FOLLOWING THE NEWS OF LINTON'S **DEPARTURE**.

THOUGH STILL AT INTERVALS SHE INQUIRED WHEN LINTON WOULD **RETURN**, BEFORE SHE **DID** SEE HIM AGAIN HIS FEATURES HAD WAXED SO **DIM** IN HER MEMORY THAT SHE DID NOT **RECOGNISE** HIM.

TIME WORE ON AT THE GRANGE IN ITS FORMER **PLEASANT** WAY TILL MISS CATHY REACHED **SIXTEEN**. ON THE ANNIVERSARY OF HER **BIRTH** WE NEVER MANIFESTED **ANY** SIGNS OF REJOICING, BECAUSE IT WAS **ALSO** THE ANNIVERSARY OF MY LATE MISTRESS'S **DEATH**.

HER FATHER **INVARIABLY** SPENT THAT DAY **ALONE**; THEREFORE CATHERINE WAS THROWN ON HER **OWN** RESOURCES FOR **AMUSEMENT**.

THIS TWENTIETH OF MARCH WAS A BEAUTIFUL SPRING DAY...

I **KNOW** WHERE I WISH TO GO; WHERE A COLONY OF **MOOR-GAME** ARE SETTLED.

THAT **MUST** BE A **GOOD** DISTANCE UP.

SHE BOUNDED **BEFORE** ME LIKE A YOUNG GREYHOUND.

WELL, **WHERE** ARE YOUR MOOR-GAME, MISS CATHY?

OH, ONLY A **LITTLE** FURTHER, ELLEN.

SHE HAD OUTSTRIPPED ME, A **LONG** WAY. WHEN I CAME IN SIGHT OF HER AGAIN...

≥GASP≤

...CATHY HAD BEEN CAUGHT ON HEATHCLIFF'S LAND, AND HE WAS **REPROVING** THE POACHER.

THOUGH YOUR **NURSE** IS IN A **HURRY**, I THINK BOTH YOU AND SHE WOULD BE THE BETTER FOR A LITTLE **REST.**

WILL YOU JUST TURN THIS NAB OF HEATH, AND WALK INTO **MY HOUSE?** YOU'LL GET HOME **EARLIER** FOR THE EASE; AND YOU SHALL RECEIVE A **KIND** WELCOME.

You mustn't, on **any** account, accede to the proposal: it is **entirely** out of the question.

WHY? I AM **TIRED** OF RUNNING, AND THE GROUND IS DEWY: I CAN'T SIT **HERE.** LET US GO, ELLEN.

MR. HEATHCLIFF, IT'S **VERY** WRONG: YOU **KNOW** YOU MEAN NO **GOOD.**

MY DESIGN IS AS **HONEST** AS POSSIBLE. I'LL INFORM YOU OF ITS **WHOLE** SCOPE. THAT THE TWO COUSINS MAY FALL IN **LOVE**, AND GET MARRIED. I'M ACTING **GENEROUSLY** TO YOUR MASTER: HIS YOUNG CHIT HAS **NO** EXPECTATIONS, AND SHOULD SHE **SECOND** MY WISHES, SHE'LL BE **PROVIDED** FOR AT ONCE AS JOINT SUCCESSOR WITH LINTON.

NOW, **WHO** IS THAT? CAN YOU **TELL?**

YOUR **SON?**

YES, YES.

LINTON, DON'T YOU **RECALL** YOUR COUSIN, THAT YOU USED TO **TEASE** US SO WITH WISHING TO **SEE?**

WHAT, LINTON! IS THAT LITTLE LINTON? HE'S TALLER THAN I AM! ARE YOU LINTON?

*THE YOUTH STEPPED FORWARD, AND **ACKNOWLEDGED** HIMSELF: SHE **KISSED** HIM FERVENTLY.*

CATHERINE ASKED HER UNCLE WHY HE DID NOT *VISIT* TO THE GRANGE WITH LINTON.

MR. LINTON HAS A PREJUDICE AGAINST ME: WE **QUARRELLED** AT ONE TIME OF OUR LIVES, WITH **UNCHRISTIAN** FEROCITY; AND, IF YOU MENTION COMING **HERE** TO HIM, HE'LL PUT A **VETO** ON YOUR VISITS ALTOGETHER.

YOU MAY COME, IF YOU **WILL**, BUT YOU **MUST** NOT MENTION IT.

WHY DID YOU QUARREL?

HE THOUGHT ME TOO **POOR** TO WED HIS **SISTER**, AND WAS **GRIEVED** THAT I GOT HER: HIS **PRIDE** WAS HURT, AND HE'LL **NEVER** FORGIVE IT.

THAT'S **WRONG!** SOME TIME I'LL **TELL** HIM SO. BUT LINTON AND I HAVE NO **SHARE** IN YOUR QUARREL. I'LL NOT COME **HERE**, THEN; HE SHALL COME TO THE **GRANGE**.

IT WILL BE TOO **FAR** FOR ME: TO WALK FOUR **MILES** WOULD **KILL** ME.

OH, I'LL ASK YOU, UNCLE – THAT IS NOT MY **COUSIN**, IS HE?

YES, YOUR MOTHER'S **NEPHEW**. DON'T YOU **LIKE** HIM? IS HE NOT A **HANDSOME** LAD?

HA! HA! HA!

YOU'LL BE THE **FAVOURITE** AMONG US, HARETON!

SHE SAYS YOU ARE A -- WHAT **WAS** IT? WELL, SOMETHING VERY FLATTERING.

HERE! YOU GO WITH HER ROUND THE FARM. AND BEHAVE LIKE A **GENTLEMAN**, MIND!

I'VE TIED HIS **TONGUE**. HE'LL NOT VENTURE A SINGLE **SYLLABLE** ALL THE TIME!

NELLY, YOU RECOLLECT ME AT HIS AGE – NAY, SOME YEARS YOUNGER. DID I EVER LOOK SO STUPID: SO "GAUMLESS," AS JOSEPH CALLS IT?

WORSE, BECAUSE MORE SULLEN WITH IT.

I'VE A PLEASURE IN HIM. HE HAS SATISFIED MY EXPECTATIONS. AND THE BEST OF IT IS, HARETON IS DAMNABLY FOND OF ME!

YOU'LL OWN THAT I'VE OUTMATCHED HINDLEY THERE. IF THE DEAD VILLAIN COULD RISE FROM HIS GRAVE TO ABUSE ME FOR HIS OFFSPRING'S WRONGS, I SHOULD HAVE THE FUN OF SEEING THE SAID OFFSPRING FIGHT HIM BACK AGAIN, INDIGNANT THAT HE SHOULD DARE TO RAIL AT THE ONE FRIEND HE HAS IN THE WORLD!

LINTON GATHERED HIS ENERGIES, LEFT THE HEARTH, AND STEPPED OUT.

WHAT IS THAT INSCRIPTION OVER THE DOOR?

IT'S SOME DAMNABLE WRITING. I CANNOT READ IT.

HA-HA! HE DOES NOT KNOW HIS LETTERS. COULD YOU BELIEVE IN THE EXISTENCE OF SUCH A COLOSSAL DUNCE?

IS HE ALL AS HE SHOULD BE? OR IS HE SIMPLE: NOT RIGHT?

I'VE QUESTIONED HIM TWICE NOW, AND EACH TIME HE LOOKED SO STUPID I THINK HE DOES NOT UNDERSTAND ME. I CAN HARDLY UNDERSTAND HIM, I'M SURE!

HEH-HEH! THERE'S NOTHING THE MATTER, BUT LAZINESS, IS THERE, EARNSHAW?

MY COUSIN FANCIES YOU ARE AN IDIOT. THERE YOU EXPERIENCE THE CONSEQUENCE OF SCORNING "BOOK-LARNING," AS YOU WOULD SAY.

HAVE YOU NOTICED, CATHERINE, HIS FRIGHTFUL YORKSHIRE PRONUNCIATION?

WHY, WHERE THE DEVIL IS THE USE ON 'T?

WE STAYED TILL *AFTERNOON*: I COULD NOT TEAR MISS CATHY *AWAY*. SHE GAVE A *FAITHFUL* ACCOUNT OF HER EXCURSION TO MY MASTER.

MR. HEATHCLIFF IS A MOST *DIABOLICAL* MAN, *DELIGHTING* TO DO WRONG AND *RUIN* THOSE HE *HATES*.

YOU WILL *KNOW* HEREAFTER, DARLING, WHY I WISH YOU TO *AVOID* HIS HOUSE AND FAMILY; NOW, THINK *NO MORE* ABOUT THEM!

IN THE EVENING I FOUND HER CRYING.

I'M NOT CRYING FOR *MYSELF*, ELLEN, IT'S FOR *LINTON*. HE EXPECTED TO *SEE* ME AGAIN TO-MORROW. MAY I NOT WRITE A *NOTE* TO TELL HIM WHY I *CANNOT* COME?

NO, INDEED! NO, *INDEED*! THEN HE WOULD WRITE TO *YOU*, AND THERE'D NEVER BE AN *END* OF IT.

NO, MISS CATHERINE, THE ACQUAINTANCE MUST BE DROPPED *ENTIRELY*: SO PAPA *EXPECTS*, AND I SHALL SEE THAT IT IS *DONE*.

SHE THREW AT ME A VERY *NAUGHTY* LOOK, *SO* NAUGHTY THAT I WOULD *NOT* KISS HER GOOD-NIGHT, AND SHUT HER DOOR, IN *GREAT* DISPLEASURE.

BUT, REPENTING HALF-WAY, I RETURNED SOFTLY, AND *LO!* THERE WAS MISS, AT THE *TABLE* WITH A BIT OF BLANK *PAPER* BEFORE HER AND A *PENCIL* IN HER HAND.

YOU'LL GET *NOBODY* TO TAKE THAT, CATHERINE, IF YOU WRITE IT;

AND AT PRESENT I SHALL PUT *OUT* YOUR CANDLE.

Pffff

SOME WEEKS AFTERWARDS, I WAS SURPRISED TO DISCOVER A *MASS* OF CORRESPONDENCE – DAILY, ALMOST IT MUST HAVE BEEN – FROM LINTON HEATHCLIFF: *ANSWERS* TO DOCUMENTS FORWARDED BY *HER*.

SO! A FINE BUNDLE OF TRASH YOU *STUDY* IN YOUR LEISURE HOURS, TO BE SURE: WHY, IT'S GOOD ENOUGH TO BE *PRINTED!*

AND WHAT DO YOU SUPPOSE THE *MASTER* WILL THINK WHEN I DISPLAY IT BEFORE *HIM? FOR SHAME!* AND YOU MUST HAVE LED THE WAY IN WRITING SUCH *ABSURDITIES:* HE WOULD NOT HAVE THOUGHT OF *BEGINNING,* I'M CERTAIN.

I DIDN'T! I *DIDN'T!*

I DIDN'T *ONCE* THINK OF LOVING HIM TILL --

LOVING! LOVING! DID ANYBODY EVER *HEAR* THE LIKE! PRETTY LOVING, *INDEED!*

AND BOTH TIMES *TOGETHER* YOU HAVE SEEN LINTON HARDLY *FOUR* HOURS IN YOUR LIFE!

NOW *HERE* IS THE BABYISH *TRASH.* I'M GOING WITH IT TO THE LIBRARY;

AND WE'LL SEE WHAT YOUR *FATHER* SAYS TO SUCH *LOVING.*

I PROMISE, ELLEN, I WILL NEITHER *SEND* NOR *RECEIVE* A LETTER *AGAIN.* OH, PUT THEM IN THE FIRE, DO, *DO!*

SPARE ONE OR *TWO,* ELLEN, TO *KEEP* FOR LINTON'S SAKE! I WILL HAVE ONE, YOU *CRUEL* WRETCH!

VERY WELL – AND I WILL HAVE SOME TO *EXHIBIT* TO PAPA!

ALL *RIGHT* – BURN THEM ALL.

NEXT MORNING I REQUESTED MASTER HEATHCLIFF TO SEND NO *MORE* NOTES TO MISS LINTON.

109

ON AN AFTERNOON IN OCTOBER, MISS CATHY **DISAPPEARED** OVER THE GRANGE GARDEN **WALL**. THE STONES WERE SMOOTH AND NEATLY CEMENTED, AND THE ROSE-BUSHES AND BLACK-BERRY STRAGGLERS COULD YIELD NO **ASSISTANCE** IN RE-ASCENDING.

ELLEN, YOU'LL HAVE TO FETCH THE **KEY**, OR ELSE I MUST RUN ROUND TO THE **PORTER'S** LODGE. I CAN'T SCALE THE RAMPARTS ON **THIS** SIDE!

STAY WHERE YOU ARE. I HAVE MY BUNDLE OF **KEYS** IN MY POCKET: PERHAPS I MAY MANAGE TO **OPEN** IT; IF NOT, I'LL GO.

HO, MISS LINTON! I'M **GLAD** TO MEET YOU. DON'T BE IN **HASTE** TO ENTER, FOR I HAVE AN **EXPLANATION** TO ASK AND OBTAIN.

I **SHA'N'T SPEAK** TO YOU, MR. HEATHCLIFF. PAPA SAYS YOU ARE A **WICKED** MAN, AND YOU HATE BOTH HIM **AND ME**; AND ELLEN SAYS THE **SAME**.

THAT IS NOTHING TO THE **PURPOSE**. I DON'T HATE MY **SON**; AND IT IS CONCERNING HIM THAT I DEMAND YOUR **ATTENTION.**

I PRESUME YOU GREW **WEARY** OF THE AMUSEMENT OF YOUR **LETTERS** TO HIM AND **DROPPED** IT. WELL, YOU DROPPED LINTON **WITH** IT, INTO A SLOUGH OF DESPOND.

HE WAS IN **EARNEST**: IN LOVE, REALLY. AS TRUE AS I LIVE, HE'S **DYING** FOR YOU; BREAKING HIS **HEART** AT YOUR **FICKLENESS**: NOT FIGURATIVELY, BUT **ACTUALLY.**

HOW CAN YOU LIE SO **GLARINGLY** TO THE POOR CHILD? PRAY **RIDE ON!** HOW CAN YOU **DELIBERATELY** GET UP SUCH PALTRY **FALSEHOODS?** MISS CATHY, I'LL KNOCK THE LOCK OFF WITH A **STONE**: YOU WON'T BELIEVE THAT VILE **NONSENSE.**

I WAS NOT AWARE THERE WERE **EAVESDROPPERS**. WORTHY MRS. DEAN, I **LIKE** YOU, BUT I **DON'T** LIKE YOUR DOUBLE-DEALING.

DON'T MIND MRS. DEAN'S **CRUEL** CAUTIONS, MISS CATHERINE; BUT BE **GENEROUS**, AND CONTRIVE TO **SEE** HIM.

HE **DREAMS** OF YOU DAY AND NIGHT, AND **CANNOT** BE PERSUADED THAT YOU DON'T **HATE** HIM, SINCE YOU NEITHER WRITE NOR **CALL**.

I **SWEAR**, ON MY SALVATION, HE'S GOING TO HIS **GRAVE**, AND NONE BUT **YOU** CAN **SAVE** HIM!

CATHERINE'S FEATURES WERE **SO** SAD, SHE EVIDENTLY REGARDED WHAT SHE HAD **HEARD** AS EVERY SYLLABLE **TRUE**.

THE NEXT DAY BEHELD ME ON THE ROAD TO *WUTHERING HEIGHTS*, BY THE SIDE OF MY WILFUL YOUNG MISTRESS'S PONY. I COULDN'T BEAR TO WITNESS HER *SORROW*: TO SEE HER PALE, DEJECTED COUNTENANCE, AND HEAVY EYES; AND I *YIELDED*, IN THE FAINT HOPE THAT LINTON *HIMSELF* MIGHT PROVE, BY HIS RECEPTION OF US, HOW LITTLE OF THE TALE WAS FOUNDED ON *FACT*.

CHAPTER XXIII

IS THAT *YOU*, MISS LINTON? DEAR ME! PAPA SAID YOU WOULD *CALL*.

WILL YOU SHUT THE *DOOR*, IF YOU PLEASE? THOSE DETESTABLE CREATURES WON'T BRING *COALS* TO THE FIRE. IT'S SO *COLD*!

AND ARE YOU *GLAD* TO SEE ME?

YES, I *AM*. IT'S SOMETHING *NEW* TO HEAR A VOICE LIKE *YOURS*! BUT I HAVE BEEN *VEXED*, BECAUSE YOU WOULDN'T *COME*.

PAPA SWORE IT WAS OWING TO *ME*: HE CALLED ME A PITIFUL, SHUFFLING, *WORTHLESS* THING; AND SAID YOU *DESPISED* ME; AND IF HE HAD BEEN IN *MY* PLACE, *HE* WOULD BE MORE THE *MASTER* OF THE GRANGE THAN YOUR *FATHER* BY THIS TIME.

BUT YOU *DON'T* DESPISE ME, DO YOU, MISS?

I WISH YOU WOULD SAY *CATHERINE*, OR *CATHY*.

DESPISE *YOU*? *NO*! NEXT TO PAPA AND ELLEN, I LOVE YOU *BETTER* THAN *ANYBODY* LIVING.

I *DON'T* LOVE MR. HEATHCLIFF, THOUGH. HE MUST BE *WICKED*, TO HAVE MADE AUNT ISABELLA *LEAVE HIM* AS SHE DID!

SHE *DIDN'T* LEAVE HIM.

SHE *DID*!

WELL, I'LL TELL **YOU** SOMETHING! YOUR MOTHER **HATED** YOUR FATHER. AND SHE **LOVED** MINE!

YOU LITTLE **LIAR**! I **HATE** YOU NOW!

SHE DID! SHE **DID**!

WOAAAH!

PUSH

=COUGH=

=COUGH=

=COUGH=

I'M SORRY I **HURT** YOU, LINTON.

BUT **I** COULDN'T HAVE BEEN HURT BY THAT LITTLE **PUSH**, AND I HAD NO IDEA THAT **YOU** COULD, EITHER: YOU'RE NOT **MUCH**, ARE YOU, LINTON?

DON'T LET ME GO HOME THINKING I'VE DONE YOU **HARM**. ANSWER! SPEAK TO ME.

I **CAN'T** SPEAK TO YOU; YOU'VE **HURT** ME SO THAT I SHALL LIE **AWAKE** ALL NIGHT CHOKING WITH THIS COUGH!

IF YOU **HAD** IT YOU'D KNOW WHAT IT WAS; BUT YOU'LL BE COMFORTABLY **ASLEEP**, WHILE I'M IN **AGONY** – AND NOBODY NEAR ME! I WONDER HOW **YOU** WOULD LIKE TO PASS THOSE **FEARFUL** NIGHTS!

BUT YOU'VE MADE YOURSELF **ILL** BY **CRYING**, AND BEING IN A **PASSION**. I DIDN'T DO IT **ALL**.

HOWEVER, WE'LL BE **FRIENDS** NOW. AND YOU WANT ME: YOU WOULD WISH TO **SEE** ME SOMETIMES, REALLY?

I **TOLD** YOU I DID. YOU MUST COME, TO **CURE** ME. YOU OUGHT TO COME, BECAUSE YOU HAVE **HURT** ME EXTREMELY! I WAS NOT AS ILL WHEN YOU ENTERED AS I AM AT **PRESENT** – WAS I?

THEY WENT ON UNTIL THE CLOCK STRUCK TWELVE. WHEN WE WERE OUT OF THE HOUSE...

DON'T YOU LIKE HIM, ELLEN?

HE'S YOUNGER THAN I, AND HE OUGHT TO LIVE THE LONGEST: HE WILL – HE MUST LIVE AS LONG AS I DO.

IT'S ONLY A COLD THAT AILS HIM, THE SAME AS PAPA HAS. YOU SAY PAPA WILL GET BETTER, AND WHY SHOULDN'T HE?

LISTEN, MISS – AND MIND, I'LL KEEP MY WORD, – IF YOU ATTEMPT GOING TO WUTHERING HEIGHTS AGAIN, WITH OR WITHOUT ME, I SHALL INFORM MR. LINTON, AND, UNLESS HE ALLOW IT, THE INTIMACY WITH YOUR COUSIN MUST NOT BE REVIVED.

LIKE HIM? THE WORST-TEMPERED BIT OF A SICKLY SLIP THAT EVER STRUGGLED INTO ITS TEENS!

HAPPILY, AS MR. HEATHCLIFF CONJECTURED, HE'LL NOT WIN TWENTY. I DOUBT WHETHER HE'LL SEE SPRING, INDEED. I'M GLAD YOU HAVE NO CHANCE OF HAVING HIM FOR A HUSBAND, MISS CATHERINE!

IT HAS BEEN REVIVED!

MUST NOT BE CONTINUED, THEN!

WE'LL SEE!

113

ON THE SUCCEEDING MORNING I WAS *LAID UP,* AND DURING THREE WEEKS I REMAINED *INCAPACITATED* FOR ATTENDING TO MY DUTIES: A CALAMITY *NEVER* EXPERIENCED *PRIOR* TO THAT PERIOD, AND NEVER, I AM THANKFUL TO SAY, *SINCE.*

MY LITTLE MISTRESS BEHAVED LIKE AN *ANGEL* IN COMING TO WAIT ON ME, AND *CHEER* MY SOLITUDE.

I GENERALLY NEEDED *NOTHING* AFTER SIX O'CLOCK, THUS THE *EVENING* WAS HER *OWN.*

AT THE CLOSE OF THREE WEEKS, I WAS ABLE TO QUIT MY *CHAMBER,* AND MOVE ABOUT THE *HOUSE.*

MY DEAR MISS CATHERINE, *WHERE* HAVE YOU BEEN RIDING OUT AT *THIS* HOUR?

WHERE HAVE YOU BEEN? *SPEAK!*

PROMISE NOT TO BE *ANGRY,* AND YOU SHALL KNOW THE VERY *TRUTH.*

CHAPTER XXIV

I'VE BEEN TO *WUTHERING HEIGHTS,* ELLEN, AND I'VE NEVER *MISSED* GOING A DAY SINCE YOU FELL ILL; EXCEPT *THRICE* BEFORE, AND TWICE AFTER YOU *LEFT* YOUR ROOM.

I WAS AT THE HEIGHTS BY HALF-PAST *SIX,* AND GENERALLY STAYED TILL HALF-PAST *EIGHT,* AND THEN *GALLOPED* HOME. IT WAS NOT TO AMUSE *MYSELF* THAT I WENT.

ONCE IN A WEEK, PERHAPS, I WAS *HAPPY.*

I'VE LEARNT TO *ENDURE* HIS SUFFERINGS.

PAPA TALKS ENOUGH OF MY *DEFECTS,* AND SHOWS ENOUGH *SCORN* OF ME, TO MAKE IT NATURAL I SHOULD *DOUBT* MYSELF.

I DOUBT WHETHER I AM NOT *ALTOGETHER* AS *WORTHLESS* AS HE CALLS ME, FREQUENTLY; AND THEN I FEEL SO *CROSS* AND *BITTER,* I HATE EVERYBODY!

I AM WORTHLESS, AND BAD IN TEMPER, AND BAD IN SPIRIT, ALMOST ALWAYS; AND, IF YOU CHOOSE, YOU MAY SAY GOOD-BYE: YOU'LL GET RID OF AN ANNOYANCE.

ONLY, CATHERINE, DO ME THIS JUSTICE: BELIEVE THAT IF I MIGHT BE AS SWEET, AND AS KIND, AND AS GOOD AS YOU ARE, I WOULD BE; AS WILLINGLY, AND MORE SO, THAN AS HAPPY AND AS HEALTHY.

AND BELIEVE THAT YOUR KINDNESS HAS MADE ME LOVE YOU DEEPER THAN IF I DESERVED YOUR LOVE:

AND THOUGH I COULDN'T, AND CANNOT HELP SHOWING MY NATURE TO YOU, I REGRET IT AND REPENT IT; AND SHALL REGRET AND REPENT IT TILL I DIE!

I FELT HE SPOKE THE TRUTH; AND I FELT I MUST FORGIVE HIM: AND, THOUGH WE SHOULD QUARREL THE NEXT MOMENT, I MUST FORGIVE HIM AGAIN. WE WERE RECONCILED.

NOW, ELLEN, YOU HAVE HEARD IT ALL; AND I CAN'T BE PREVENTED FROM GOING TO WUTHERING HEIGHTS, EXCEPT BY INFLICTING MISERY ON TWO PEOPLE; WHEREAS, IF YOU'LL ONLY NOT TELL PAPA, MY GOING NEED DISTURB THE TRANQUILLITY OF NONE.

YOU'LL NOT TELL, WILL YOU? IT WILL BE VERY HEARTLESS, IF YOU DO.

I'LL MAKE UP MY MIND ON THAT POINT BY TO-MORROW, MISS CATHERINE. IT REQUIRES SOME STUDY; AND SO I'LL LEAVE YOU TO YOUR REST, AND GO THINK IT OVER.

I THOUGHT IT OVER ALOUD, IN MY MASTER'S PRESENCE. MR. LINTON WAS ALARMED AND DISTRESSED MORE THAN HE WOULD ACKNOWLEDGE TO ME.

IN THE MORNING, CATHERINE LEARNT MY BETRAYAL OF HER CONFIDENCE, AND SHE LEARNT ALSO THAT HER SECRET VISITS TO WUTHERING HEIGHTS WERE TO END.

CHAPTER XXV

THESE THINGS HAPPENED LAST **WINTER**, SIR, HARDLY MORE THAN A **YEAR** AGO.

LAST WINTER, I DID NOT **THINK**, AT ANOTHER TWELVE MONTHS' **END**, I SHOULD BE AMUSING A **STRANGER** TO THE FAMILY WITH RELATING THEM!

YET, WHO KNOWS HOW LONG **YOU'LL** BE A STRANGER? YOU'RE TOO **YOUNG** TO REST **ALWAYS** CONTENTED, LIVING BY **YOURSELF**; AND I SOME WAY FANCY **NO ONE** COULD SEE CATHERINE LINTON AND **NOT** LOVE HER.

YOU **SMILE**; BUT WHY DO YOU LOOK SO **LIVELY** AND **INTERESTED** WHEN I **TALK** ABOUT HER?

STOP, MY GOOD FRIEND!

IT MAY BE **VERY** POSSIBLE THAT I **SHOULD** LOVE HER; BUT WOULD **SHE** LOVE **ME**?

I **DOUBT** IT TOO MUCH TO VENTURE MY **TRANQUILLITY** BY RUNNING INTO **TEMPTATION**: AND THEN MY **HOME** IS NOT HERE. I'M OF THE **BUSY WORLD**, AND TO ITS ARMS I MUST **RETURN**.

GO ON. WAS CATHERINE **OBEDIENT** TO HER FATHER'S **COMMANDS**?

SHE WAS.

HER AFFECTION FOR HIM WAS STILL THE **CHIEF** SENTIMENT IN HER HEART; AND HE SPOKE WITHOUT **ANGER**, AS ONE ABOUT TO LEAVE HIS **TREASURE** AMID **PERILS** AND **FOES**.

I WISH MY NEPHEW WOULD **WRITE**, ELLEN, OR **CALL**. TELL ME, **SINCERELY**, WHAT YOU THINK OF HIM: IS HE CHANGED FOR THE **BETTER**, OR IS THERE A PROSPECT OF **IMPROVEMENT**, AS HE GROWS A **MAN**?

HE'S VERY **DELICATE**, SIR, AND SCARCELY LIKELY TO **REACH** MANHOOD: BUT THIS I **CAN** SAY, HE DOES **NOT** RESEMBLE HIS **FATHER**;

AND IF MISS CATHERINE HAD THE MISFORTUNE TO **MARRY** HIM, HE WOULD NOT BE BEYOND HER **CONTROL**.

ELLEN, I'VE BEEN **VERY** HAPPY WITH MY LITTLE CATHY. THROUGH WINTER NIGHTS AND SUMMER DAYS SHE WAS A LIVING **HOPE** AT MY SIDE.

BUT I'VE BEEN AS HAPPY MUSING BY **MYSELF** AMONG THOSE **STONES**, UNDER THAT OLD **CHURCH**: LYING, THROUGH THE LONG JUNE EVENINGS, ON THE GREEN MOUND OF HER MOTHER'S **GRAVE**, AND WISHING, **YEARNING** FOR THE TIME WHEN I MIGHT LIE **BENEATH** IT.

WHAT CAN I DO FOR **CATHY**?

I'D NOT CARE ONE **MOMENT** FOR LINTON BEING **HEATHCLIFF'S** SON; NOR FOR HIS TAKING HER **FROM** ME, IF HE COULD CONSOLE HER FOR MY **LOSS**.

I'D NOT **CARE** THAT HEATHCLIFF GAINED HIS ENDS, AND **TRIUMPHED** IN ROBBING ME OF MY **LAST** BLESSING!

BUT SHOULD LINTON BE **UNWORTHY** – ONLY A FEEBLE **TOOL** TO HIS FATHER – I **CANNOT** ABANDON HER TO HIM!

I'D RATHER RESIGN HER TO **GOD**, AND LAY HER IN THE **EARTH** BEFORE **ME**.

RESIGN HER TO **GOD** AS IT **IS**, SIR, AND IF WE SHOULD LOSE **YOU** --

– WHICH MAY **HE** FORBID –

UNDER **HIS** PROVIDENCE, I'LL STAND HER FRIEND AND COUNSELLOR TO THE **LAST**.

MISS CATHERINE IS A **GOOD** GIRL; I DON'T FEAR THAT SHE WILL GO **WILFULLY** WRONG; AND PEOPLE WHO DO THEIR **DUTY** ARE ALWAYS **FINALLY** REWARDED.

SPRING ADVANCED; YET MY MASTER GATHERED NO **REAL** STRENGTH, THOUGH HE RESUMED HIS **WALKS** IN THE GROUNDS WITH HIS DAUGHTER.

TO HER INEXPERIENCED NOTIONS, THIS ITSELF WAS A SIGN OF **CONVALESCENCE**; AND THEN HIS CHEEK WAS OFTEN FLUSHED, AND HIS EYES WERE BRIGHT; SHE FELT **SURE** OF HIS **RECOVERING**.

LINTON WROTE TO MY MASTER. MR. HEATHCLIFF **OBJECTED** TO HIS **CALLING** AT THE GRANGE; AND, AS MR. LINTON **FORBADE** CATHERINE FROM GOING TO WUTHERING HEIGHTS, LINTON PLEADED ELOQUENTLY FOR THEM TO **MEET** ON HER **RIDE**.

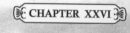

CHAPTER XXVI

SUMMER WAS **ALREADY** PAST ITS PRIME, WHEN EDGAR **RELUCTANTLY** YIELDED HIS ASSENT TO CATHERINE'S **ENTREATIES** TO SEE HER COUSIN.

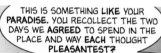

WHEN WE REACHED LINTON, AND THAT WAS SCARCELY A **QUARTER** OF A MILE FROM HIS OWN **DOOR**, WE FOUND HE HAD NO **HORSE**; AND WE WERE FORCED TO **DISMOUNT** AND LEAVE OURS TO **GRAZE**.

WHY, MASTER HEATHCLIFF, YOU ARE NOT **FIT** FOR ENJOYING A **RAMBLE** THIS MORNING.

HOW **ILL** YOU DO LOOK!

YOU HAVE BEEN **WORSE** THAN WHEN I SAW YOU **LAST** – YOU ARE **THINNER**, AND –

I'M **TIRED**. IT IS TOO **HOT** FOR WALKING, LET US REST **HERE**.

THIS IS SOMETHING **LIKE** YOUR **PARADISE**. YOU RECOLLECT THE TWO DAYS WE **AGREED** TO SPEND IN THE PLACE AND WAY **EACH** THOUGHT **PLEASANTEST?**

THIS IS **NEARLY** YOURS, ONLY THERE ARE **CLOUDS;** BUT THEN THEY ARE SO **SOFT** AND **MELLOW:** IT IS **NICER** THAN SUNSHINE.

NEXT WEEK, IF YOU **CAN**, WE'LL **RIDE** DOWN TO THE GRANGE PARK, AND TRY **MINE**.

LINTON DID NOT APPEAR TO **REMEMBER** WHAT SHE TALKED OF; AND HE HAD EVIDENTLY GREAT **DIFFICULTY** IN SUSTAINING **ANY** KIND OF **CONVERSATION**.

CATHERINE PERCEIVED, AS WELL AS **I** DID, THAT HE HELD IT RATHER A **PUNISHMENT**, THAN A **GRATIFICATION**, TO **ENDURE** OUR COMPANY; AND SHE MADE NO SCRUPLE OF PROPOSING, PRESENTLY, TO **DEPART**. THAT PROPOSAL, UNEXPECTEDLY, **ROUSED** LINTON FROM HIS LETHARGY, AND THREW HIM INTO A STRANGE STATE OF **AGITATION**.

PLEASE REMAIN ANOTHER **HALF-HOUR**, AT LEAST.

119

SEVEN DAYS GLIDED AWAY, EVERY ONE MARKING ITS COURSE BY THE HENCEFORTH *RAPID* ALTERATION OF EDGAR LINTON'S *STATE*. WE DEFERRED OUR EXCURSION TILL THE *AFTERNOON*.

IT IS **LATE**! IS NOT YOUR FATHER **VERY** ILL? I THOUGHT YOU WOULDN'T COME.

CHAPTER XXVII

MY FATHER IS VERY ILL; AND WHY AM I **CALLED** FROM HIS **BEDSIDE**? WHY DIDN'T YOU SEND TO **ABSOLVE** ME FROM MY **PROMISE**, WHEN YOU WISHED I WOULDN'T **KEEP** IT?

COME! I DESIRE AN *EXPLANATION*: PLAYING AND TRIFLING ARE COMPLETELY *BANISHED* OUT OF MY MIND; AND I CAN'T **DANCE ATTENDANCE** ON YOUR AFFECTATIONS *NOW!*

MY **AFFECTATIONS!** WHAT ARE **THEY?** FOR HEAVEN'S SAKE, CATHERINE, DON'T LOOK SO **ANGRY!** DESPISE ME AS **MUCH** AS YOU PLEASE; I AM A WORTHLESS, COWARDLY **WRETCH:** I CAN'T BE SCORNED **ENOUGH!**

BUT I'M TOO **MEAN** FOR YOUR **ANGER** – HATE MY FATHER, AND **SPARE** ME – FOR CONTEMPT.

NONSENSE! FOOLISH, **SILLY** BOY!

AND THERE! HE **TREMBLES:** AS IF I WERE **REALLY** GOING TO **TOUCH** HIM! YOU NEEDN'T BESPEAK **CONTEMPT**, LINTON:

I SHALL RETURN **HOME**.

OH! I CANNOT **BEAR** IT! CATHERINE, *CATHERINE*, I'M A TRAITOR, **TOO**, AND I **DARE** NOT TELL YOU!

BUT **LEAVE** ME, AND I SHALL BE **KILLED!** DEAR CATHERINE, MY LIFE IS IN **YOUR** HANDS.

AND PERHAPS YOU **WILL** CONSENT – AND HE'LL LET ME **DIE** WITH **YOU!**

CONSENT TO **WHAT?** TO STAY? TELL ME THE **MEANING** OF THIS STRANGE TALK, AND I **WILL**. YOU **CONTRADICT** YOUR **OWN** WORDS, AND **DISTRACT** ME.

BUT MY FATHER **THREATENED** ME, AND I DREAD HIM – I DREAD HIM! I DARE NOT TELL!

OH WELL! **KEEP** YOUR **SECRET** – **I'M** NOT AFRAID!

IT IS SOMETHING TO SEE YOU SO **NEAR** TO MY **HOUSE**, NELLY!

HOW ARE YOU AT THE **GRANGE**? LET US HEAR. THE RUMOUR GOES THAT **EDGAR LINTON** IS ON HIS **DEATH-BED**.

PERHAPS THEY **EXAGGERATE** HIS ILLNESS?

NO; MY MASTER IS **DYING**: IT IS **TRUE** ENOUGH.

A **SAD** THING IT WILL BE FOR US ALL, BUT A **BLESSING** FOR HIM!

HALLO! HAS THE WHELP BEEN PLAYING **THAT** GAME LONG? I DID GIVE HIM SOME **LESSONS** ABOUT SNIVELLING.

IS HE PRETTY **LIVELY** WITH MISS **LINTON** GENERALLY?

LIVELY? NO – HE HAS SHOWN THE GREATEST **DISTRESS**.

TO SEE HIM, I SHOULD SAY, THAT INSTEAD OF **RAMBLING** WITH HIS SWEETHEART ON THE **HILLS**, HE OUGHT TO BE IN **BED**, UNDER THE HANDS OF A DOCTOR.

HE **SHALL** BE, IN A DAY OR TWO. BUT FIRST –

GET **UP**, LINTON! **GET UP**! DON'T GROVEL ON THE GROUND THERE – UP, THIS **MOMENT**!

I'M GETTING **ANGRY**. DAMN YOU! GET UP, **DIRECTLY**!

MISS LINTON: BE SO **KIND** AS TO WALK **HOME** WITH HIM, WILL YOU?

HE **SHUDDERS** IF I TOUCH HIM.

LINTON, DEAR! I **CAN'T** GO TO WUTHERING HEIGHTS: PAPA HAS **FORBIDDEN** ME. HE'LL NOT **HARM** YOU: WHY ARE YOU SO **AFRAID**?

I CAN **NEVER** RE-ENTER THAT HOUSE. I'M **NOT** TO RE-ENTER IT WITHOUT **YOU**!

STOP! WE'LL RESPECT CATHERINE'S FILIAL SCRUPLES.

PLEASE – I IMPLORE YOU!

HOWEVER I DISAPPROVED, I COULDN'T *HINDER* HER: INDEED, HOW COULD SHE HAVE *REFUSED* HIM HERSELF?

WHAT WAS FILLING HIM WITH DREAD WE HAD NO MEANS OF *DISCERNING;* BUT THERE HE WAS, *POWERLESS* UNDER ITS *GRIP.*

MY HOUSE IS NOT STRICKEN WITH THE **PLAGUE,** NELLY; AND I HAVE A MIND TO BE **HOSPITABLE** TO-DAY: SIT DOWN, AND ALLOW ME TO SHUT THE **DOOR.**

HE SHUT AND *LOCKED* IT ALSO. I STARTED.

YOU SHALL HAVE **TEA** BEFORE YOU GO HOME. I AM BY **MYSELF.**

MISS LINTON, TAKE YOUR SEAT BY **HIM.** HOW SHE **DOES** STARE! IT'S ODD WHAT A **SAVAGE** FEELING I HAVE TO ANYTHING THAT SEEMS AFRAID OF ME!

HAD I BEEN BORN WHERE LAWS ARE LESS **STRICT,** AND TASTES LESS **DAINTY,** I SHOULD TREAT MYSELF TO A SLOW **VIVISECTION** OF THOSE TWO, AS AN EVENING'S **AMUSEMENT.**

BY *HELL!*

I *HATE* THEM.

SLAM

I AM **NOT** AFRAID OF **YOU!** GIVE ME THAT **KEY:** I WILL HAVE IT!

I WOULDN'T EAT OR DRINK HERE, IF I WERE **STARVING.**

HEATHCLIFF HAD THE KEY IN HIS *HAND*. HE LOOKED AT CATHERINE, SEIZED WITH A SORT OF *SURPRISE* AT HER *BOLDNESS;*

OR, POSSIBLY, *REMINDED,* BY HER VOICE AND GLANCE, OF THE PERSON FROM WHOM SHE *INHERITED* IT.

NOW, CATHERINE LINTON, STAND *OFF,* OR I SHALL KNOCK YOU *DOWN;* AND, THAT WILL MAKE MRS. DEAN *MAD.*

WE WILL GO!

WE WILL GO!

HAH!

!!!

SLAP

123

YOU VILLAIN!

YOU VILLAIN!

I KNOW HOW TO CHASTISE CHILDREN, YOU SEE.

I SHALL BE YOUR FATHER, TO-MORROW –

ALL THE FATHER YOU'LL HAVE IN A FEW DAYS –

AND YOU SHALL HAVE PLENTY OF THAT.

YOU CAN BEAR PLENTY – YOU'RE NO WEAKLING – YOU SHALL HAVE A DAILY TASTE, IF I CATCH SUCH A DEVIL OF A TEMPER IN YOUR EYES AGAIN!

WASH AWAY YOUR SPLEEN, AND HELP YOUR OWN NAUGHTY PET AND MINE. IT IS NOT POISONED, THOUGH I PREPARED IT.

I'M GOING **OUT** TO SEEK YOUR **HORSES**.

OUR **FIRST** THOUGHT, ON HIS DEPARTURE, WAS TO FORCE AN **EXIT** SOMEWHERE.

WE TRIED THE KITCHEN DOOR, BUT THAT WAS **FASTENED** OUTSIDE; AND THE WINDOWS WERE TOO **NARROW** FOR EVEN **CATHY'S** LITTLE FIGURE.

WE WERE REGULARLY **IMPRISONED**.

MASTER LINTON, YOU **KNOW** WHAT YOUR DIABOLICAL FATHER IS **AFTER**, AND YOU SHALL **TELL** US, OR I'LL **BOX** YOUR EARS, AS **HE** HAS DONE YOUR **COUSIN'S**.

GIVE ME SOME **TEA**, I'M THIRSTY, AND THEN I'LL **TELL** YOU.

CATHERINE, YOU ARE LETTING YOUR **TEARS** FALL INTO MY **CUP**! I WON'T DRINK **THAT**. GIVE ME **ANOTHER**.

CATHERINE PUSHED **ANOTHER** TO HIM.

PAPA WANTS US TO BE **MARRIED**. AND HE KNOWS **YOUR** PAPA WOULDN'T **LET** US MARRY NOW; AND HE'S AFRAID OF MY **DYING** IF WE **WAIT**.

SO WE ARE TO BE MARRIED IN THE **MORNING**, AND YOU ARE TO STAY HERE ALL **NIGHT**; AND, IF YOU DO AS HE **WISHES**, YOU SHALL RETURN **HOME** NEXT DAY, AND TAKE ME **WITH** YOU.

TAKE **YOU** WITH HER, PITIFUL CHANGELING? YOU **MARRY?** WHY, THE MAN IS **MAD!** OR HE THINKS US **FOOLS**, EVERY ONE.

AND DO YOU **IMAGINE** THAT **BEAUTIFUL** YOUNG LADY, THAT HEALTHY, **HEARTY** GIRL, WILL **TIE** HERSELF TO A LITTLE PERISHING **MONKEY** LIKE YOU?

NOW, LINTON! SNIVELLING **AGAIN**? WHAT HAS SHE BEEN **DOING** TO YOU?

COME, COME – HAVE DONE, AND GET TO **BED**. IN A **MONTH** OR TWO, MY LAD, YOU'LL BE ABLE TO PAY HER **BACK** HER **PRESENT** TYRANNIES, WITH A **VIGOROUS** HAND.

I'LL LOOK TO THE **REST**.

MR. **HEATHCLIFF**, LET ME GO **HOME**! PAPA WILL BE **MISERABLE**. I **PROMISE** TO MARRY LINTON: PAPA WOULD **LIKE** ME TO: AND I **LOVE** HIM –

AND WHY SHOULD YOU WISH TO **FORCE** ME TO DO WHAT I'LL **WILLINGLY** DO OF MYSELF?

LET HIM **DARE** TO FORCE YOU. THERE'S **LAW** IN THE LAND, THANK **GOD**!

THERE IS; THOUGH WE BE IN AN OUT-OF-THE-WAY PLACE. I'D **INFORM**, IF HE WERE MY OWN SON: AND IT'S **FELONY** WITHOUT BENEFIT OF **CLERGY**!

SILENCE!

TO THE DEVIL WITH YOUR **CLAMOUR**!

MISS LINTON, I SHALL **ENJOY** MYSELF **REMARKABLY** IN THINKING YOUR FATHER WILL BE **MISERABLE**: I SHALL NOT **SLEEP** FOR **SATISFACTION**. YOU COULD HAVE HIT ON NO **SURER** WAY OF **FIXING** YOUR RESIDENCE UNDER **MY** ROOF, FOR THE NEXT TWENTY-FOUR HOURS, THAN INFORMING ME THAT **SUCH** AN EVENT WOULD **FOLLOW**.

AS TO YOUR **PROMISE** TO MARRY LINTON, I'LL TAKE CARE YOU SHALL **KEEP** IT; FOR YOU SHALL **NOT** QUIT THIS PLACE TILL IT IS **FULFILLED**.

NELLY, SHE MUST EITHER **ACCEPT** HIM OR REMAIN A **PRISONER**, AND **YOU** ALONG WITH HER, TILL YOUR MASTER DIES.

I CAN **DETAIN** YOU **BOTH**, QUITE CONCEALED, HERE. IF YOU **DOUBT**, ENCOURAGE HER TO **RETRACT** HER WORD, AND YOU'LL HAVE AN OPPORTUNITY OF **JUDGING**!

I'LL **NOT** RETRACT MY WORD. I'LL MARRY HIM, WITHIN THIS **HOUR**, IF I MAY GO TO THRUSHCROSS GRANGE **AFTERWARDS.**

MR. HEATHCLIFF, YOU'RE A **CRUEL** MAN, BUT YOU'RE **NOT** A FIEND; AND YOU WON'T, FROM MERE **MALICE**, DESTROY, IRREVOCABLY, **ALL** MY HAPPINESS.

I DON'T **HATE** YOU. I'M NOT **ANGRY** THAT YOU **STRUCK** ME. HAVE YOU **NEVER** LOVED **ANYBODY** IN ALL YOUR **LIFE**, UNCLE? **NEVER?**

I'M SO WRETCHED, YOU CAN'T **HELP** BEING SORRY AND **PITYING** ME.

KEEP YOUR EFT'S FINGERS **OFF;** AND **MOVE**, OR I'LL **KICK** YOU!

I'D RATHER BE HUGGED BY A **SNAKE.** HOW THE DEVIL CAN YOU **DREAM** OF FAWNING ON ME? I DETEST YOU!

IT WAS GROWING **DARK.**

WE HEARD THE SOUND OF **VOICES** AT THE **GARDEN GATE.** OUR HOST HURRIED **OUT** INSTANTLY.

HE HAD HIS *WITS* ABOUT HIM; WE HAD *NOT*.

I thought it had been your cousin *Hareton*. I *wish* he would arrive! Who knows but he might take *our* part?

IT WAS THREE *SERVANTS* SENT TO *SEEK* YOU FROM THE GRANGE.

YOU SHOULD HAVE OPENED A *LATTICE* AND CALLED *OUT*: BUT I COULD *SWEAR* THAT CHIT IS GLAD YOU *DIDN'T*.

SHE'S *GLAD* TO BE OBLIGED TO *STAY*, I'M CERTAIN.

OH *NO!*

≶SOB≷ ≶SOB≷

AT LEARNING THE *CHANCE* WE HAD *MISSED*, WE BOTH GAVE VENT TO OUR *GRIEF* WITHOUT CONTROL.

AT NINE O'CLOCK, HE BADE US GO *UPSTAIRS* TO ZILLAH'S CHAMBER. WE NEITHER OF US LAY DOWN: CATHERINE TOOK HER *STATION* BY THE LATTICE, AND WATCHED *ANXIOUSLY* FOR *MORNING*.

AT SEVEN O'CLOCK HEATHCLIFF CAME, AND *PULLED* MISS LINTON *OUT*. I ROSE TO *FOLLOW*, BUT HE TURNED THE *LOCK* AGAIN.

AND THERE I *REMAINED* ENCLOSED. *FIVE NIGHTS* AND *FOUR DAYS* I REMAINED, SEEING *NOBODY* BUT HARETON, ONCE EVERY MORNING; AND HE WAS A *MODEL* OF A JAILER: SURLY, AND DUMB, AND *DEAF* TO EVERY ATTEMPT AT MOVING HIS SENSE OF *JUSTICE* OR *COMPASSION*.

ON THE FIFTH MORNING, OR RATHER *AFTERNOON,* A *DIFFERENT* STEP APPROACHED. IT WAS *ZILLAH.*

EH, DEAR! MRS. DEAN! THERE IS A *TALK* ABOUT YOU AT GIMMERTON.

I NEVER THOUGHT BUT YOU WERE *SUNK* IN THE *BLACKHORSE* MARSH, AND MISSY *WITH* YOU, TILL *MASTER* TOLD ME YOU'D BEEN *FOUND,* AND HE'D LODGED YOU *HERE!*

⟪ CHAPTER XXVIII ⟫

DID MASTER *SAVE* YOU?

YOUR *MASTER* IS A *TRUE SCOUNDREL!* BUT HE SHALL *ANSWER* FOR IT.

HE *NEEDN'T* HAVE RAISED THAT *TALE:* IT SHALL *ALL* BE LAID BARE!

I HASTENED BELOW.

WHERE IS MISS CATHERINE? IS SHE *GONE?*

NO; SHE'S *UPSTAIRS:* SHE'S NOT TO GO; WE WON'T *LET* HER.

YOU WON'T *LET* HER, LITTLE *IDIOT!*

SHE'S *MY WIFE,* AND SHE *SHAN'T* GO HOME!

HAVE YOU *FORGOTTEN* ALL CATHERINE'S *KINDNESS* TO YOU LAST WINTER, WHEN YOU AFFIRMED YOU *LOVED* HER, AND WHEN SHE BROUGHT YOU *BOOKS* AND SUNG YOU *SONGS,* AND CAME *MANY* A TIME THROUGH *WIND* AND SNOW TO SEE *YOU?*

AND *NOW* YOU BELIEVE THE *LIES* YOUR FATHER TELLS, THOUGH YOU KNOW HE *DETESTS* YOU *BOTH!* AND YOU JOIN HIM *AGAINST* HER.

THAT'S *FINE* GRATITUDE, IS IT NOT? IS MR. *HEATHCLIFF* OUT?

HE'S IN THE COURT, TALKING TO *DOCTOR KENNETH* WHO SAYS UNCLE IS *DYING.* I'M GLAD, FOR I SHALL BE *MASTER* OF THE GRANGE *AFTER* HIM.

CATHERINE ALWAYS SPOKE OF IT AS *HER* HOUSE. IT *ISN'T* HERS! IT'S *MINE:* PAPA SAYS *EVERYTHING* SHE HAS IS MINE.

SHE *OFFERED* TO GIVE ME *EVERYTHING* IF I WOULD LET HER *OUT;* BUT I TOLD HER SHE HAD *NOTHING* TO GIVE, THEY WERE ALL, ALL MINE.

YOU CAN GET THE *KEY* IF YOU *CHOOSE?* IN WHAT *APARTMENT* IS IT?

OH, I *SHAN'T* TELL YOU WHERE IT IS! IT IS OUR *SECRET.*

THERE! YOU'VE *TIRED* ME – GO AWAY, GO *AWAY!*

I CONSIDERED IT BEST TO **DEPART,** AND BRING A **RESCUE** FOR MY YOUNG LADY, FROM THE GRANGE.

ON REACHING IT, THE **ASTONISHMENT** OF MY FELLOW SERVANTS TO SEE ME WAS **INTENSE.**

HOW **CHANGED** I FOUND MR. EDGAR, EVEN IN THOSE **FEW DAYS!** HE LAY AN IMAGE OF **SADNESS,** AND **RESIGNATION,** WAITING HIS **DEATH.**

HE **DIVINED** THAT HIS ENEMY'S **PURPOSE** WAS TO SECURE THE PERSONAL **PROPERTY,** AS WELL AS THE **ESTATE,** TO HIS SON, OR RATHER **HIMSELF.**

HE FELT THAT HIS **WILL** HAD BETTER BE **ALTERED:** HE DETERMINED TO PUT CATHERINE'S **FORTUNE** IN THE HANDS OF **TRUSTEES,** FOR USE DURING HER LIFE. BY THAT MEANS, IT COULD **NOT** FALL TO **MR. HEATHCLIFF.**

HAVING **RECEIVED** HIS ORDERS, I **DESPATCHED** A MAN TO FETCH THE **ATTORNEY,** AND **FOUR** MORE, PROVIDED WITH SERVICEABLE **WEAPONS,** TO **DEMAND** MY YOUNG LADY OF HER **JAILER.**

THE SINGLE SERVANT RETURNED **FIRST.** MR. GREEN, THE LAWYER, WAS **OUT,** BUT HE WOULD BE AT THE GRANGE IN THE **MORNING.**

THE FOUR MEN CAME BACK **UNACCOMPANIED.** THEY BROUGHT WORD THAT CATHERINE WAS **ILL:** TOO ILL TO QUIT HER **ROOM;** AND HEATHCLIFF WOULD NOT SUFFER THEM TO **SEE** HER.

I **SCOLDED** THE STUPID FELLOWS **WELL** FOR **LISTENING** TO THAT TALE, WHICH I WOULD **NOT** CARRY TO MY MASTER; RESOLVING TO TAKE A WHOLE **BEVY** UP TO THE HEIGHTS, AT DAY-LIGHT, AND **STORM** IT, **LITERALLY,** UNLESS THE PRISONER WERE QUIETLY **SURRENDERED** TO US.

HAPPILY, I WAS **SPARED** THE JOURNEY AND THE TROUBLE. I HAD GONE **DOWN-STAIRS** AT THREE O'CLOCK TO FETCH A JUG OF WATER, WHEN...

?!?

knock knock knock

ELLEN, ELLEN!

IS PAPA **ALIVE?**

YES, **YES,** MY ANGEL, HE **IS.** GOD BE THANKED, YOU ARE **SAFE** WITH US AGAIN!

SHE WANTED TO **RUN,** BREATHLESS AS SHE WAS, UPSTAIRS TO **MR. LINTON'S** ROOM;

I **IMPLORED** HER TO SAY SHE SHOULD BE **HAPPY** WITH **YOUNG HEATHCLIFF.** SHE **STARED,** BUT SOON COMPREHENDING **WHY** I COUNSELLED HER TO UTTER THE **FALSEHOOD,** SHE **ASSURED** ME SHE WOULD NOT **COMPLAIN.**

CATHERINE'S **DESPAIR** WAS AS **SILENT** AS HER FATHER'S **JOY.** SHE **SUPPORTED** HIM CALMLY, IN APPEARANCE; AND HE **FIXED** ON HER FEATURES HIS RAISED **EYES** THAT SEEMED DILATING WITH **ECSTASY.**

I am going to her;

and **you,** darling child, **shall** come to us!

HE NEVER **STIRRED** OR **SPOKE** AGAIN;

BUT **CONTINUED** THAT RAPT, RADIANT GAZE...

...TILL HIS PULSE IMPERCEPTIBLY **STOPPED,** AND HIS SOUL **DEPARTED.**

NONE COULD HAVE NOTICED THE **EXACT** MINUTE OF HIS **DEATH...**

...IT WAS SO ENTIRELY WITHOUT A **STRUGGLE.**

AT DINNER-TIME APPEARED THE **LAWYER,** HAVING CALLED AT **WUTHERING HEIGHTS** TO GET HIS INSTRUCTIONS HOW TO **BEHAVE.**

HE HAD **SOLD** HIMSELF TO MR. **HEATHCLIFF,** AND **THAT** WAS THE CAUSE OF HIS **DELAY** IN OBEYING MY MASTER'S **SUMMONS.**

FORTUNATELY, NO **THOUGHT** OF **WORLDLY** AFFAIRS CROSSED THE LATTER'S MIND, TO **DISTURB** HIM, AFTER HIS **DAUGHTER'S** ARRIVAL.

CHAPTER XXIX

THE EVENING AFTER THE *FUNERAL*, MY *YOUNG LADY* AND I WERE SEATED IN THE *LIBRARY*, WHEN *HEATHCLIFF* ARRIVED.

HE MADE NO CEREMONY OF *KNOCKING*, OR ANNOUNCING HIS *NAME*: HE WAS *MASTER*, AND AVAILED HIMSELF OF THE MASTER'S *PRIVILEGE* TO WALK *STRAIGHT IN*, WITHOUT SAYING A *WORD*.

HE ENTERED THE *LIBRARY*. IT WAS THE *SAME* ROOM INTO WHICH HE HAD BEEN USHERED, AS A *GUEST*, EIGHTEEN YEARS *BEFORE*: THE SAME MOON SHONE THROUGH THE WINDOW; AND THE SAME AUTUMN LANDSCAPE LAY *OUTSIDE*.

NO *MORE* RUNNINGS AWAY! WHERE WOULD YOU *GO*?

I'M COME TO FETCH YOU *HOME*; AND I HOPE YOU'LL BE A *DUTIFUL* DAUGHTER AND NOT ENCOURAGE MY *SON* TO FURTHER DISOBEDIENCE.

I WAS *EMBARRASSED* HOW TO *PUNISH* HIM, WHEN I DISCOVERED HIS *PART* IN THE BUSINESS.

SINCE THEN, MY *PRESENCE* IS AS *POTENT* ON HIS NERVES AS A *GHOST*. WHETHER YOU LIKE YOUR PRECIOUS MATE, OR *NOT*, YOU *MUST* COME: HE'S *YOUR* CONCERN NOW; I YIELD *ALL* MY INTEREST IN HIM TO *YOU*.

WHY NOT LET CATHERINE CONTINUE *HERE*? AND SEND MASTER LINTON *TO* HER?

AS YOU *HATE* THEM *BOTH*, YOU'D NOT *MISS* THEM: THEY CAN ONLY BE A DAILY *PLAGUE* TO YOUR *UNNATURAL* HEART.

I'M SEEKING A *TENANT* FOR THE *GRANGE*, AND I WANT MY CHILDREN *ABOUT* ME, TO BE SURE – BESIDES, *THAT* LASS *OWES* ME HER *SERVICES* FOR HER *BREAD*; I'M NOT GOING TO NURTURE HER IN *LUXURY* AND *IDLENESS* AFTER LINTON IS *GONE*.

MAKE *HASTE* AND GET *READY* NOW; AND DON'T OBLIGE ME TO *COMPEL* YOU.

I SHALL. LINTON IS ALL I **HAVE** TO LOVE IN THE WORLD. I KNOW HE HAS A **BAD** NATURE: HE'S **YOUR** SON. BUT I'M GLAD I'VE A **BETTER**, TO **FORGIVE** IT; AND I KNOW HE LOVES **ME**, AND FOR **THAT** REASON I LOVE **HIM**.

MR. HEATHCLIFF, YOU HAVE **NOBODY** TO LOVE YOU; AND, **HOWEVER** MISERABLE YOU MAKE US, WE SHALL STILL HAVE THE **REVENGE** OF THINKING THAT **YOUR** CRUELTY ARISES FROM YOUR **GREATER** MISERY!

YOU **ARE** MISERABLE, ARE YOU NOT? LONELY, LIKE THE **DEVIL**, AND **ENVIOUS** LIKE HIM?

YOU SHALL BE **SORRY** TO BE **YOURSELF** PRESENTLY, IF YOU STAND THERE ANOTHER **MINUTE**.

BEGONE, **WITCH**, AND GET YOUR **THINGS**.

NOBODY LOVES YOU — **NOBODY** WILL CRY FOR YOU WHEN YOU **DIE**!

I **WOULDN'T** BE **YOU**!

YOU KNOW, I WAS **WILD** AFTER CATHY **DIED**; AND **ETERNALLY**, FROM DAWN TO DAWN, PRAYING HER TO **RETURN** TO ME — HER **SPIRIT** — I HAVE A STRONG FAITH IN **GHOSTS**; I HAVE A **CONVICTION** THAT THEY CAN, AND **DO** EXIST, AMONG **US**!

THE DAY SHE WAS **BURIED**, IN THE EVENING, I GOT A **SPADE** FROM THE TOOL-HOUSE, AND BEGAN TO **DELVE** WITH ALL MY MIGHT — IT SCRAPED THE **COFFIN**.

*I'LL HAVE HER IN MY **ARMS** AGAIN! IF SHE BE COLD, I'LL THINK IT IS THIS NORTH WIND THAT **CHILLS** ME; AND IF SHE BE **MOTIONLESS**, IT IS **SLEEP**.*

CATHERIN
LINTO

I WAS ON THE POINT OF **ATTAINING** MY OBJECT, WHEN IT SEEMED THAT I HEARD A **SIGH** FROM SOME ONE **ABOVE**.

THERE WAS **ANOTHER** SIGH, CLOSE AT MY EAR. I APPEARED TO FEEL THE WARM BREATH OF IT **DISPLACING** THE WIND. I KNEW NO **LIVING** THING IN FLESH AND BLOOD WAS BY; BUT I FELT THAT **CATHY** WAS **THERE**: NOT **UNDER** ME, BUT **ON** THE EARTH. HER **PRESENCE** WAS **WITH** ME: IT **REMAINED** WHILE I RE-FILLED THE GRAVE, AND LED ME **HOME**.

I HAVE PAID A VISIT TO THE HEIGHTS, BUT I HAVE NOT SEEN HER SINCE SHE LEFT. JOSEPH WOULDN'T LET ME PASS THE DOOR. ZILLAH HAS TOLD ME SOMETHING OF THE WAY THEY GO ON, OTHERWISE I SHOULD HARDLY KNOW WHO WAS DEAD AND WHO LIVING.

ZILLAH SAID MRS. LINTON WENT STRAIGHT TO LINTON'S ROOM WHEN SHE ARRIVED AT THE HEIGHTS.

CHAPTER XXX

MIGHT YOU SEND FOR A DOCTOR? LINTON IS VERY ILL.

WE KNOW THAT! BUT HIS LIFE IS NOT WORTH A FARTHING, AND I WON'T SPEND A FARTHING ON HIM.

IF NOBODY WILL HELP ME, HE'LL DIE!

NONE HERE CARE WHAT BECOMES OF HIM; IF YOU DO, ACT THE NURSE; IF YOU DO NOT, LOCK HIM UP AND LEAVE HIM.

AT LAST, ONE NIGHT, SHE WAS SURE LINTON WAS DYING. MR. HEATHCLIFF WENT UP, LOOKED AT HIM, AND TOUCHED HIM.

NOW, CATHERINE – HOW DO YOU FEEL?

HE'S SAFE, AND I'M FREE.

I SHOULD FEEL WELL – BUT YOU HAVE LEFT ME SO LONG TO STRUGGLE AGAINST DEATH, ALONE, THAT I FEEL AND SEE ONLY DEATH! I FEEL LIKE DEATH!

HEATHCLIFF SHOWED HER LINTON'S WILL. HE HAD BEQUEATHED THE WHOLE OF HIS, AND WHAT HAD BEEN HER MOVEABLE PROPERTY TO HIS FATHER.

THE POOR CREATURE WAS THREATENED, OR COAXED, INTO THE ACT DURING HER WEEK'S ABSENCE, WHEN HIS UNCLE DIED.

CATHERINE, DESTITUTE OF CASH AND FRIENDS, CANNOT DISTURB HIS POSSESSION.

THUS **ENDED** MRS. DEAN'S STORY. NOTWITHSTANDING THE DOCTOR'S **PROPHECY**, I AM RAPIDLY RECOVERING **STRENGTH**;

AND, THOUGH IT BE ONLY THE SECOND WEEK IN **JANUARY**, I PROPOSE GETTING OUT ON **HORSEBACK** IN A DAY OR TWO, AND **RIDING** OVER TO WUTHERING HEIGHTS, TO **INFORM** MY LANDLORD THAT I SHALL SPEND THE NEXT SIX MONTHS IN **LONDON**;

AND, IF HE **LIKES**, HE MAY LOOK OUT FOR **ANOTHER** TENANT TO TAKE THE PLACE, AFTER OCTOBER – I WOULD NOT PASS **ANOTHER** WINTER HERE FOR **MUCH**.

CHAPTER XXXI

I SHALL SET OUT FOR LONDON, **NEXT** WEEK; AND I MUST GIVE YOU WARNING, THAT I FEEL **NO** DISPOSITION TO **RETAIN** THRUSHCROSS GRANGE BEYOND THE TWELVE-MONTHS I **AGREED** TO RENT IT.

I BELIEVE I SHALL **NOT** LIVE THERE ANY MORE.

OH, INDEED; YOU'RE **TIRED** OF BEING **BANISHED** FROM THE WORLD, ARE YOU MR. LOCKWOOD? BUT, IF YOU BE COMING TO PLEAD OFF **PAYING** FOR A PLACE YOU WON'T OCCUPY, YOUR JOURNEY IS **USELESS**: I NEVER RELENT IN EXACTING MY **DUE**, FROM ANY ONE.

I'M COMING TO PLEAD OFF **NOTHING** ABOUT IT. SHOULD YOU **WISH** IT, I'LL SETTLE WITH YOU **NOW**.

NO, NO. TAKE YOUR **DINNER** WITH US.

WITH MR. HEATHCLIFF, **GRIM** AND **SATURNINE**, AND HARETON, ABSOLUTELY **DUMB**, I MADE A SOMEWHAT **CHEERLESS** MEAL, AND BID ADIEU **EARLY**.

HOW **DREARY** LIFE GETS OVER IN THAT **HOUSE!** WHAT A REALISATION OF SOMETHING MORE **ROMANTIC** THAN A **FAIRY TALE** IT WOULD HAVE BEEN FOR MRS. LINTON HEATHCLIFF, HAD **SHE AND I** STRUCK UP AN **ATTACHMENT**, AS HER GOOD NURSE **DESIRED**.

CHAPTER XXXII

1802 – THIS SEPTEMBER, I WAS INVITED TO DEVASTATE THE **MOORS** OF A FRIEND, IN THE NORTH; AND, ON MY JOURNEY TO HIS ABODE, I UNEXPECTEDLY CAME WITHIN FIFTEEN MILES OF **GIMMERTON**. A SUDDEN **IMPULSE** SEIZED ME TO VISIT **THRUSHCROSS GRANGE**.

I CONCEIVED THAT I MIGHT AS WELL PASS THE NIGHT UNDER MY **OWN** ROOF, AS IN AN INN. BESIDES, I COULD SPARE A DAY EASILY, TO ARRANGE MATTERS WITH MY **LANDLORD**, AND THUS SAVE MYSELF THE TROUBLE OF INVADING THE NEIGHBOURHOOD AGAIN.

IS MRS. DEAN WITHIN?

NAY! SHOO DOESN'T BIDE **HERE**; SHOO'S UP AT TH' **HEIGHTS**.

WUTHERING HEIGHTS WAS THE **GOAL** OF MY PROPOSED EXCURSION.

THE **GATE** AT THE HEIGHTS YIELDED TO MY HAND. I COULD BOTH SEE AND HEAR THE **INMATES** TALK BEFORE I **ENTERED**, AND LOOKED AND LISTENED IN CONSEQUENCE; BEING MOVED THERETO BY A MINGLED SENSE OF **CURIOSITY**, AND **ENVY** THAT **GREW** AS I LINGERED.

CON-**TRARY**! THAT FOR THE **THIRD** TIME, YOU DUNCE! I'M NOT GOING TO **TELL** YOU AGAIN – **RECOLLECT**, OR I'LL PULL YOUR HAIR!

CONTRARY, THEN.

AND NOW, **KISS** ME, FOR MINDING SO WELL.

NO, READ IT **OVER** FIRST **CORRECTLY**, WITHOUT A **SINGLE** MISTAKE.

THE TASK WAS **DONE**, NOT FREE FROM FURTHER BLUNDERS; BUT THE PUPIL CLAIMED A **REWARD**, AND RECEIVED AT LEAST **FIVE** KISSES: WHICH, HOWEVER, HE **GENEROUSLY** RETURNED.

I JUDGED THEY WERE ABOUT TO ISSUE **OUT** AND HAVE A **WALK** ON THE MOORS.

I SKULKED ROUND TO SEEK REFUGE IN THE **KITCHEN**. THERE WAS NO UNOBSTRUCTED ADMITTANCE ON THAT SIDE.

WHY, **BLESS** YOU, MR. LOCKWOOD! HOW COULD YOU **THINK** OF RETURNING IN THIS WAY?

ALL'S **SHUT UP** AT THRUSHCROSS GRANGE. YOU SHOULD HAVE GIVEN US **NOTICE**.

BUT, STEP **IN**, PRAY! HAVE YOU **WALKED** FROM GIMMERTON THIS EVENING?

FROM THE **GRANGE**; AND, WHILE THEY MAKE ME LODGING ROOM THERE, I WANT TO **FINISH** MY BUSINESS WITH YOUR **MASTER**; BECAUSE I DON'T THINK OF HAVING **ANOTHER** OPPORTUNITY IN A HURRY.

WHAT BUSINESS, SIR? HE'S GONE **OUT** AT PRESENT, AND WON'T RETURN **SOON**.

ABOUT THE **RENT**.

OH! THEN IT IS WITH **MRS.** HEATHCLIFF YOU MUST SETTLE; OR RATHER WITH **ME**.

SHE HAS NOT LEARNT TO **MANAGE** HER AFFAIRS YET, AND I ACT **FOR** HER: THERE'S NOBODY ELSE.

AH! YOU HAVE NOT HEARD OF HEATHCLIFF'S **DEATH**, I SEE.

HEATHCLIFF **DEAD?**

HOW LONG AGO?

THREE MONTHS SINCE: BUT, SIT DOWN, AND LET ME TAKE YOUR HAT, AND I'LL TELL YOU ALL ABOUT IT.

I WAS SUMMONED TO WUTHERING HEIGHTS, WITHIN A FORTNIGHT OF YOUR LEAVING US.

I AM SICK OF SEEING CATHERINE: YOU MUST MAKE THE LITTLE PARLOUR YOUR SITTING ROOM, AND KEEP HER WITH YOU.

IN THE BEGINNING, SHE SHUNNED REMARKING OR ADDRESSING HARETON. HE WAS ALWAYS AS SULLEN AND SILENT AS POSSIBLE.

AFTER A WHILE, SHE CHANGED HER BEHAVIOUR, AND WOULD COMMENT ON HIS STUPIDITY AND IDLENESS. SHE WAS SORRY FOR HIS PERSEVERING SULKINESS: HER CONSCIENCE REPROVED HER FOR FRIGHTENING HIM OFF IMPROVING HIMSELF.

HER INGENUITY WAS AT WORK TO REMEDY THE INJURY: WHILE I IRONED, SHE WOULD READ ALOUD TO ME, AND WOULD LEAVE THE BOOK LYING ABOUT FOR HARETON: THAT SHE DID REPEATEDLY; BUT HE WAS AS OBSTINATE AS A MULE.

YOU SHOULD BE FRIENDS WITH YOUR COUSIN, MR. HARETON, SINCE SHE REPENTS OF HER SAUCINESS!

IT WOULD DO YOU A GREAT DEAL OF GOOD: IT WOULD MAKE YOU ANOTHER MAN TO HAVE HER FOR A COMPANION.

A COMPANION? WHEN SHE HATES ME, AND DOES NOT THINK ME FIT TO WIPE HER SHOON!

NAY, IF IT MADE ME A KING, I'D NOT BE SCORNED FOR SEEKING HER GOOD-WILL ANY MORE.

IT IS NOT I WHO HATE YOU, IT IS YOU WHO HATE ME! YOU HATE ME AS MUCH AS MR. HEATHCLIFF DOES, AND MORE.

YOU'RE A DAMNED LIAR: WHY HAVE I MADE HIM ANGRY, BY TAKING YOUR PART, THEN, A HUNDRED TIMES?

AND THAT WHILE YOU SNEERED AT AND DESPISED ME.

I DIDN'T KNOW YOU TOOK MY PART; AND I WAS **MISERABLE** AND **BITTER** AT EVERYBODY;

BUT, NOW I **THANK** YOU, AND **BEG** YOU TO **FORGIVE** ME: WHAT CAN I DO BESIDES?

CATHERINE, BY INSTINCT, IMPRESSED ON HIS CHEEK A GENTLE **KISS**.

I SHOOK MY HEAD REPROVINGLY.

WELL! WHAT **SHOULD** I HAVE DONE, ELLEN? HE WOULDN'T SHAKE **HANDS**, AND HE WOULDN'T **LOOK**:

I MUST SHOW HIM **SOME** WAY THAT I **LIKE** HIM – THAT I WANT TO BE **FRIENDS**.

I OVERHEARD NO FURTHER DISTINGUISHABLE TALK, BUT, ON LOOKING ROUND LATER, I PERCEIVED TWO SUCH **RADIANT** COUNTENANCES BENT OVER THE PAGE OF THE **BOOK**, THAT I DID NOT DOUBT THE **TREATY** HAD BEEN **RATIFIED**, ON BOTH SIDES; AND THE **ENEMIES** WERE, THENCE FORTH, SWORN **ALLIES**.

THE INTIMACY THUS **COMMENCED**, GREW **RAPIDLY**. YOU SEE, MR. LOCKWOOD, IT WAS EASY **ENOUGH** TO WIN MRS. HEATHCLIFF'S HEART. I'M GLAD YOU DID NOT **TRY**. THE CROWN OF **ALL** MY WISHES WILL BE THE **UNION** OF THOSE TWO.

ON THE MORROW, CATHERINE PERSUADED EARNSHAW TO *CLEAR* A LARGE *SPACE* OF GROUND FROM BUSHES FOR A *FLOWER BED.*

I WAS *TERRIFIED* AT THE *DEVASTATION;* THE BUSHES WERE THE APPLE OF *JOSEPH'S* EYE.

CHAPTER XXXIII

JOSEPH WAS *FURIOUS;* AS WAS *MR. HEATHCLIFF.*

WHO THE **DEVIL** GAVE **YOU** LEAVE TO TOUCH A **STICK** ABOUT THE **PLACE?**

AND WHO ORDERED **YOU** TO **OBEY** HER?

YOU SHOULDN'T GRUDGE A FEW YARDS OF **EARTH** FOR ME TO **ORNAMENT,** WHEN **YOU** HAVE **TAKEN** ALL MY LAND!

YOUR LAND, INSOLENT **SLUT?** YOU NEVER **HAD** ANY!

AND MY MONEY, AND HARETON'S LAND, AND **HIS** MONEY. HARETON AND I ARE **FRIENDS** NOW; AND I SHALL TELL HIM **ALL** ABOUT YOU!

IF YOU **STRIKE** ME, HARETON WILL STRIKE **YOU,** SO YOU MAY AS WELL **SIT DOWN.**

IF HARETON DOES NOT TURN **YOU** OUT OF THE ROOM, I'LL STRIKE **HIM** TO HELL.

DAMNABLE WITCH!

DARE YOU PRETEND TO ROUSE HIM AGAINST **ME?**

OFF WITH HER! DO YOU **HEAR?** FLING HER INTO THE KITCHEN!

I'LL **KILL** HER, ELLEN DEAN, IF YOU LET HER COME INTO MY **SIGHT** AGAIN!

WISHT! WISHT! I WILL NOT HEAR YOU SPEAK SO TO HIM. HAVE DONE.

BUT YOU WON'T LET HIM STRIKE ME?

ACCURSED WITCH!

THIS TIME SHE HAS **PROVOKED** ME WHEN I COULD NOT **BEAR** IT; AND I'LL MAKE HER **REPENT** IT FOR **EVER.**

GRRAH!

ARGH!

HE SEEMED READY TO **TEAR** CATHERINE TO **PIECES.**

GASP

WHEN OF A SUDDEN, HIS FINGERS **RELAXED.**

YOU **MUST** LEARN TO **AVOID** PUTTING ME IN A **PASSION,** OR I SHALL **REALLY MURDER** YOU SOME TIME!

AS TO **HARETON EARNSHAW,** IF I SEE HIM **LISTEN** TO YOU, I'LL SEND HIM SEEKING HIS **BREAD** WHERE HE CAN **GET** IT! **YOUR** LOVE WILL MAKE HIM AN **OUTCAST,** AND A BEGGAR.

LEAVE ME, ALL OF YOU! *LEAVE* ME!

LATER THAT DAY...

IT IS A **POOR** CONCLUSION, IS IT NOT? MY OLD **ENEMIES** HAVE **NOT** BEATEN ME;

NOW WOULD BE THE **PRECISE** TIME TO **REVENGE** MYSELF ON THEIR REPRESENTATIVES. BUT WHERE IS THE **USE?**

I HAVE **LOST** THE FACULTY OF ENJOYING THEIR **DESTRUCTION,** AND I AM TOO **IDLE** TO DESTROY FOR **NOTHING.**

NELLY, THERE IS A STRANGE **CHANGE** APPROACHING: I'M IN ITS **SHADOW** AT PRESENT.

I CANNOT LOOK **DOWN** TO THIS FLOOR, BUT **HER** FEATURES ARE SHAPED IN THE **FLAGS!** IN EVERY OBJECT, I AM **SURROUNDED** WITH HER **IMAGE!**

THE ENTIRE **WORLD** IS A DREADFUL **COLLECTION** OF **MEMORANDA** THAT SHE DID **EXIST,** AND THAT I HAVE **LOST** HER!

143

WHAT DO YOU **MEAN** BY A **CHANGE**, MR. **HEATHCLIFF**? YOU HAVE NO FEELING OF **ILLNESS**, HAVE YOU?

NO, I HAVE NOT.

THEN, YOU ARE NOT **AFRAID** OF **DEATH**?

AFRAID? **NO!** I HAVE A **SINGLE** WISH, AND MY WHOLE **BEING** AND **FACULTIES** ARE **YEARNING** TO ATTAIN IT.

THEY HAVE **YEARNED** TOWARDS IT SO **LONG**, AND SO **UNWAVERINGLY**, THAT I'M **CONVINCED** IT WILL BE REACHED – AND **SOON** – BECAUSE IT HAS **DEVOURED** MY EXISTENCE: I AM SWALLOWED UP IN THE **ANTICIPATION** OF ITS **FULFILMENT**.

O, **GOD!** IT IS A **LONG** FIGHT; I WISH IT WERE **OVER!**

CONSCIENCE HAD TURNED HIS HEART TO AN EARTHLY **HELL**.

FOR SOME DAYS AFTER THAT EVENING, MR. HEATHCLIFF **SHUNNED** MEETING US AT **MEALS**, CHOOSING RATHER TO **ABSENT** HIMSELF.

CHAPTER XXXIV

ONE NIGHT, AFTER THE FAMILY WERE IN BED, I **HEARD** HIM GO **OUT**. IN THE MORNING I FOUND HE WAS **STILL AWAY**.

MR. HEATHCLIFF IS COMING IN. HE LOOKS **DIFFERENT**.

HOW?

WHY, ALMOST **BRIGHT** AND **CHEERFUL**. NO – VERY MUCH **EXCITED**, AND WILD, AND **GLAD!**

NIGHT-WALKING **AMUSES** HIM, THEN.

HEATHCLIFF STOOD AT THE OPEN **DOOR**;

HE WAS PALE, AND HE **TREMBLED**: YET, CERTAINLY, HE HAD A STRANGE **JOYFUL** GLITTER IN HIS **EYES**, THAT ALTERED THE **ASPECT** OF HIS WHOLE **FACE**.

WILL YOU HAVE SOME **BREAKFAST**? YOU MUST BE **HUNGRY**, RAMBLING ABOUT ALL **NIGHT!**

I DON'T THINK IT **RIGHT** TO WANDER OUT OF **DOORS** INSTEAD OF BEING IN BED.

144

LAST NIGHT I WAS ON THE **THRESHOLD** OF HELL. TO-DAY, I AM WITHIN SIGHT OF MY **HEAVEN.** I HAVE MY **EYES** ON IT: HARDLY **THREE FEET** TO SEVER ME!

AND NOW YOU'D BETTER **GO!** YOU'LL NEITHER **SEE** NOR **HEAR** ANYTHING TO FRIGHTEN YOU, IF YOU **REFRAIN** FROM PRYING.

LEAVE ME **ALONE:** GET IN, AND DON'T **ANNOY** ME.

HE DID NOT QUIT THE HOUSE AGAIN THAT AFTERNOON, AND NO ONE **INTRUDED** ON HIS **SOLITUDE;** TILL, AT EIGHT O'CLOCK, I DEEMED IT **PROPER,** THOUGH **UNSUMMONED,** TO CARRY A CANDLE AND HIS **SUPPER** TO HIM.

MR. **HEATHCLIFF,** SIR?

MR. **HEATHCLIFF!**

MASTER!

DON'T, FOR **GOD'S SAKE,** STARE AS IF YOU SAW AN **UNEARTHLY** VISION.

DON'T, FOR **GOD'S SAKE,** SHOUT SO **LOUD.** TURN ROUND, AND **TELL** ME, ARE WE BY **OURSELVES?**

OF COURSE; OF **COURSE** WE ARE!

145

NOW, I PERCEIVED HE WAS **NOT** LOOKING **AT** THE WALL; IT SEEMED EXACTLY THAT HE GAZED AT SOMETHING WITHIN **TWO YARDS'** DISTANCE. AND WHATEVER IT WAS, IT **COMMUNICATED,** APPARENTLY, BOTH **PLEASURE** AND **PAIN** IN EXQUISITE EXTREMES: AT LEAST, THE **ANGUISHED,** YET **RAPTURED** EXPRESSION OF HIS COUNTENANCE **SUGGESTED** THAT IDEA.

HE MUTTERED DETACHED **WORDS** ALSO; THE ONLY ONE I COULD **CATCH** WAS THE NAME OF **CATHERINE,** COUPLED WITH SOME **WILD** TERM OF ENDEARMENT OR SUFFERING; AND **SPOKEN** AS ONE WOULD SPEAK TO A PERSON **PRESENT;** LOW AND EARNEST, AND WRUNG FROM THE **DEPTH** OF HIS **SOUL.**

Oh, Catherine... Catherine!

THE NEXT MORNING, HE **CALLED** TO ME.

NELLY, COME **HERE** – IS IT **MORNING?** COME IN WITH YOUR **LIGHT.**

WHEN DAY BREAKS I'LL SEND FOR **GREEN;** I WISH TO MAKE SOME **LEGAL** INQUIRIES OF HIM WHILE I CAN BESTOW A **THOUGHT** ON THOSE MATTERS, AND WHILE I CAN ACT **CALMLY.**

I HAVE NOT WRITTEN MY **WILL** YET; AND HOW TO LEAVE MY **PROPERTY** I CANNOT **DETERMINE!** I WISH I COULD **ANNIHILATE** IT FROM THE FACE OF THE **EARTH.**

I WOULD NOT **TALK** SO, MR. HEATHCLIFF.

LET YOUR WILL **BE,** A WHILE: YOU'LL BE **SPARED** TO **REPENT** OF YOUR **MANY** INJUSTICES, YET!

DO TAKE SOME **FOOD,** AND SOME **REPOSE.** YOU NEED ONLY **LOOK** AT YOURSELF IN A GLASS TO SEE HOW YOU REQUIRE **BOTH.** YOUR CHEEKS ARE **HOLLOW,** AND YOUR EYES **BLOODSHOT,** LIKE A PERSON **STARVING** WITH HUNGER, AND GOING **BLIND** WITH LOSS OF SLEEP.

IT IS NOT MY FAULT THAT I CANNOT **EAT** OR REST.

WELL, NEVER MIND MR. GREEN. I'VE DONE NO INJUSTICE, AND I REPENT OF NOTHING. I'M TOO HAPPY; AND YET I'M NOT HAPPY ENOUGH. MY SOUL'S BLISS KILLS MY BODY, BUT DOES NOT SATISFY ITSELF.

HAPPY, MASTER? STRANGE HAPPINESS! IF YOU WOULD HEAR ME WITHOUT BEING ANGRY, I MIGHT OFFER SOME ADVICE THAT WOULD MAKE YOU HAPPIER.

WHAT IS THAT? GIVE IT.

YOU ARE AWARE, MR. HEATHCLIFF, THAT FROM THE TIME YOU WERE THIRTEEN YEARS OLD, YOU HAVE LIVED A SELFISH, UNCHRISTIAN LIFE; AND PROBABLY HARDLY HAD A BIBLE IN YOUR HANDS DURING ALL THAT PERIOD.

COULD IT BE HURTFUL TO SEND FOR SOME ONE – SOME MINISTER OF ANY DENOMINATION, IT DOES NOT MATTER WHICH, TO EXPLAIN IT, AND SHOW YOU HOW UNFIT YOU WILL BE FOR ITS HEAVEN, UNLESS A CHANGE TAKES PLACE BEFORE YOU DIE?

I'M RATHER OBLIGED THAN ANGRY, NELLY, FOR YOU REMIND ME OF THE MANNER THAT I DESIRE TO BE BURIED IN.

NO MINISTER NEED COME; NOR NEED ANYTHING BE SAID OVER ME – I TELL YOU, I HAVE NEARLY ATTAINED MY HEAVEN; AND THAT OF OTHERS IS ALTOGETHER UNVALUED AND UNCOVETED BY ME!

I BELIEVE YOU THINK ME A FIEND! I'LL NOT HURT YOU. NO! TO YOU, I'VE MADE MYSELF WORSE THAN THE DEVIL.

WELL, THERE IS ONE WHO WON'T SHRINK FROM MY COMPANY! BY GOD! SHE'S RELENTLESS.

OH, DAMN IT! IT'S UNUTTERABLY TOO MUCH FOR FLESH AND BLOOD TO BEAR – EVEN MINE.

HE SOLICITED THE SOCIETY OF NO ONE MORE. AT DUSK, HE WENT INTO HIS CHAMBER. THROUGH THE WHOLE NIGHT, AND FAR INTO THE MORNING, WE HEARD HIM GROANING AND MURMURING TO HIMSELF.

147

THE FOLLOWING EVENING WAS VERY **WET:** INDEED IT **POURED** DOWN, TILL DAY-DAWN; AND, AS I TOOK MY MORNING WALK ROUND THE HOUSE, I OBSERVED THE MASTER'S **WINDOW** SWINGING **OPEN,** AND THE RAIN DRIVING STRAIGHT **IN.**

HE CANNOT BE IN **BED:** THOSE SHOWERS WOULD DRENCH HIM **THROUGH.** HE MUST EITHER BE **UP** OR **OUT.** I'LL GO BOLDLY AND **LOOK!**

MR. HEATHCLIFF WAS **THERE** – LAID ON HIS BACK. HIS **EYES** MET MINE SO **KEEN** AND **FIERCE,** I **STARTED;** AND THEN HE SEEMED TO **SMILE.**

I COULD NOT THINK HIM **DEAD:** BUT HIS FACE AND THROAT WERE **WASHED** WITH RAIN; THE BED-CLOTHES **DRIPPED,** AND HE WAS PERFECTLY **STILL.**

ONE HAND WAS GRAZED; NO **BLOOD** TRICKLED FROM THE BROKEN SKIN, AND WHEN I PUT MY FINGERS TO IT, I COULD **DOUBT** NO MORE:

HE WAS **DEAD** AND **STARK!**

I TRIED TO CLOSE HIS **EYES:** TO EXTINGUISH, IF POSSIBLE, THAT FRIGHTFUL, LIFE-LIKE **GAZE** OF **EXULTATION,** BEFORE ANY ONE **ELSE** BEHELD IT.

THEY WOULD NOT **SHUT:** THEY SEEMED TO **SNEER** AT MY ATTEMPTS; AND HIS PARTED LIPS AND SHARP WHITE TEETH **SNEERED TOO!**

TAKEN WITH ANOTHER FIT OF *COWARDICE*, I CRIED OUT FOR *JOSEPH*. HE SHUFFLED UP AND MADE A NOISE, BUT RESOLUTELY *REFUSED* TO *MEDDLE* WITH HIM.

TH' DIVIL'S HARRIED OFF HIS *SOUL*, AND HE MUH HEV' HIS *CARCASS* INTUH T' BARGIN, FOR OW'T AW CARE! ECH! WHAT A *WICKED* 'UN HE LOOKS, GIRNNING AT *DEATH*!

I FELT *STUNNED* BY THE *AWFUL* EVENT; AND MY *MEMORY* UNAVOIDABLY *RECURRED* TO FORMER TIMES WITH A SORT OF *OPPRESSIVE* SADNESS.

BUT POOR *HARETON*, THE *MOST* WRONGED, WAS THE ONLY ONE WHO *REALLY* SUFFERED MUCH. HE SAT BY THE CORPSE *ALL NIGHT*, *WEEPING* IN BITTER EARNEST.

HE PRESSED ITS *HAND*, AND KISSED THE SARCASTIC, *SAVAGE* FACE THAT EVERY ONE ELSE *SHRANK* FROM CONTEMPLATING; AND *BEMOANED* HIM WITH THAT STRONG *GRIEF* WHICH SPRINGS *NATURALLY* FROM A *GENEROUS* HEART, THOUGH IT BE *TOUGH* AS TEMPERED *STEEL*.

WE BURIED HIM, TO THE *SCANDAL* OF THE *WHOLE* NEIGHBOURHOOD, AS HE HAD *WISHED*, NEXT TO HIS *CATHY*.

BUT THE COUNTRY FOLKS WOULD *SWEAR* ON THEIR BIBLE THAT HE *WALKS*: IDLE *TALES*, YOU'LL SAY, AND SO SAY I. YET THAT OLD MAN BY THE KITCHEN FIRE *AFFIRMS* HE HAS SEEN *TWO* ON 'EM LOOKING OUT OF HIS CHAMBER WINDOW, ON *EVERY* RAINY NIGHT SINCE HIS *DEATH*.

I DON'T LIKE BEING LEFT BY **MYSELF** IN THIS **GRIM** HOUSE: I CANNOT HELP IT; I SHALL BE **GLAD** WHEN THEY LEAVE IT, AND SHIFT TO THE **GRANGE.**

THEY ARE GOING TO THE **GRANGE,** THEN?

YES, AS SOON AS THEY ARE **MARRIED;** AND THAT WILL BE ON **NEW YEAR'S DAY.**

THEY ARE AFRAID OF **NOTHING.** TOGETHER, THEY WOULD BRAVE **SATAN** AND ALL HIS **LEGIONS.**

I FELT **IRRESISTIBLY** IMPELLED TO **ESCAPE** THEM AGAIN; AND, PRESSING MY **REMEMBRANCE** INTO THE **HAND** OF MRS. DEAN, I **VANISHED** THROUGH THE KITCHEN AS THEY OPENED THE HOUSE **DOOR.**

MY WALK HOME WAS **LENGTHENED** BY A **DIVERSION** IN THE DIRECTION OF THE **KIRK.** I SOUGHT, AND SOON **DISCOVERED,** THE THREE **HEADSTONES**...

...AND I WONDERED HOW **ANYONE** COULD EVER IMAGINE **UNQUIET** SLEEPERS IN THAT QUIET **EARTH.**

Wuthering Heights

The End

Emily Brontë

(1818 –1848)

© National Portrait Gallery, London.

Emily Jane Brontë was born on July 30, 1818, at 74 Market Street in the village of Thornton near Bradford, Yorkshire. She was the fifth of six children born to Maria Branwell and Patrick Brontë, the others being Maria (1814), Elizabeth (1815), Charlotte (1816), Patrick Branwell (who was known as "Branwell," 1817) and Anne (1820).

Emily's father, Patrick, was a clergyman and writer, born in County Down, Ireland, in 1777. His surname was originally Brunty, but he decided to change it, probably to make people think he came from a more well-to-do and sophisticated background, giving the world the now famous "Brontë" name. He became a teacher in 1798, and a clergyman in 1807. In 1812, he became an examiner at a school in Guiseley, near Leeds.

Her mother, Maria, was born in Cornwall in 1785 to a prosperous merchant family. She met her future husband in Guiseley while visiting her aunt and uncle. They married in December 1812, and first lived in Hightown for three years before moving to Thornton, where Emily was born.

In April 1820 the family moved a short distance from Thornton to Haworth, where Patrick had been appointed curate of the church. They moved into The Parsonage next to the church (now the home of the Brontë Parsonage Museum: www.bronte.org.uk).

A year later, Emily's Aunt Elizabeth joined them at The Parsonage to help look after the children and also to care for Emily's mother, who was now in the final stages of cancer. Sadly, Maria Brontë died within a few months, in September 1821, when Emily was just three years old.

Because of Patrick's work, the Parsonage at Howarth was a literary household, with a large library of books. From early childhood, the Brontë children wrote their own fiction, capturing the lives, wars and sufferings of people who lived in imaginary kingdoms. The story goes that Branwell received some toy soldiers in June 1826, and the children used these as inspiration. Charlotte and Branwell wrote stories about the country they created, which they called "Angria," while Emily and Anne wrote articles and poems about their imaginary country, "Gondal." These sagas, plays, poems and stories were written down in handmade "little books" — books that they had made themselves from paper sheets stitched together.

In July 1824 Maria (10) and Elizabeth (9) were sent away to the Clergy Daughter's School at Cowan Bridge, near Kirkby Lonsdale in Lancashire. Charlotte (8) and Emily (6) later joined them there in August. Life at the boarding school must have been grim. Maria became ill and was sent home in February 1825; she died at Haworth in May. Elizabeth fell ill that same month and, like her sister, was sent home, dying just a few months later. Both died from tuberculosis (also known as "consumption"), and as a result of their deaths, Emily and

Charlotte were withdrawn from the school and educated at home by their father and their aunt Elizabeth.

Aged 20, Emily became a teacher at Law Hill School in Halifax. The post required her to work incredibly long days, and it affected her health, forcing her to leave employment after only a few months and return home. Three years later, in 1842, Emily traveled to Brussels with her sister Charlotte, to study at the Pensionnat Heger — a boarding school run by Constantin Heger and his wife. Emily's Aunt Elizabeth paid for this trip, with the plan that they would set up their own school at the Parsonage when they returned. However, the girls had to return to England later that year when their Aunt Elizabeth died at the age of 66.

The sisters finally began their project to start a school of their own. Unfortunately, this turned out to be a total failure — they didn't manage to enroll a single student!

However, this was probably to the world's advantage. The sisters had continued to write throughout the years, and in 1846 — having abandoned the idea of starting a school — they decided to publish a selection of their poems. They funded the publication themselves: one thousand copies of their book, simply entitled *Poems* were printed, at a cost to the sisters of around £50. The book received some favorable reviews, but sold only two copies in the first year.

It was not published under their own names, but under pseudonyms: Currer (Charlotte), Ellis (Emily) and Acton (Anne) Bell.

Charlotte gave an explanation for these names:

> "Averse to personal publicity, we veiled our own names under those of Currer, Ellis and Acton Bell; the ambiguous choice being dictated by a sort of conscientious scruple at assuming Christian names positively masculine, while we did not like to declare ourselves women, because - without at that time suspecting that our mode of writing and thinking was not what is called 'feminine' - we had a vague impression that authoresses are liable to be looked on with prejudice; we had noticed how critics sometimes use for their chastisement the weapon of personality, and for their reward, a flattery, which is not true praise."

A year later, in 1847, all three living sisters published their individual masterpieces, again under their assumed "Bell" names. Emily published *Wuthering Heights* as a two-volume story in a three-volume set, the third volume being Anne's *Agnes Grey*; Charlotte's book of that notable year was, of course, *Jane Eyre*.

What would have been a happy episode in the sisters' lives soon turned to tragedy. Their brother, Branwell, had been subjecting himself to alcohol and opium abuse for many years, and in 1848 he died — officially from tuberculosis, thought to be brought on by his drug and drink habits. He was just thirty-one years old.

Around the same time, Anne and Emily both fell ill, also with tuberculosis. One theory for the family's poor health was the unsanitary conditions at home, brought about by water contamination from the graveyard that was right next to the Parsonage.

Emily died on December 19, 1848, aged just thirty. Anne died five months later in May 1849, aged twenty-nine. Charlotte lived the longest, but only until 1855, when she also died from tuberculosis at the age of thirty-nine. None of the sisters had any children. Their father outlived them all, finally passing away in June 1861 at the age of eighty-four.

Sadly, Emily did not even live long enough to see her book published under her own name, which didn't happen until Charlotte edited and published the work as a singular novel in 1850. Initially, the book received a mixed reception. Many critics found it too difficult and intricate a story. In hindsight, of course, the book was simply ahead of its time.

Today, *Wuthering Heights* is considered a masterpiece of English literature and regarded by many as their favorite classic novel, inspiring numerous other books (most notably being its inclusion within Stephenie Meyer's *Twilight* series), movies, parodies, and music, including a UK number one single in 1978 by Kate Bush. Even the names themselves of Cathy and Heathcliff have become synonymous with timeless passion and a love that never dies.

It is both remarkable and sad that *Wuthering Heights* was Emily's first and only novel, containing, as it does, unusually vast depths of emotion, incredibly complex characters, and a fascinating storyline set over a long period of time. It is a truly monumental masterpiece from an author cursed with tragedy.

The Brontë Family Tree

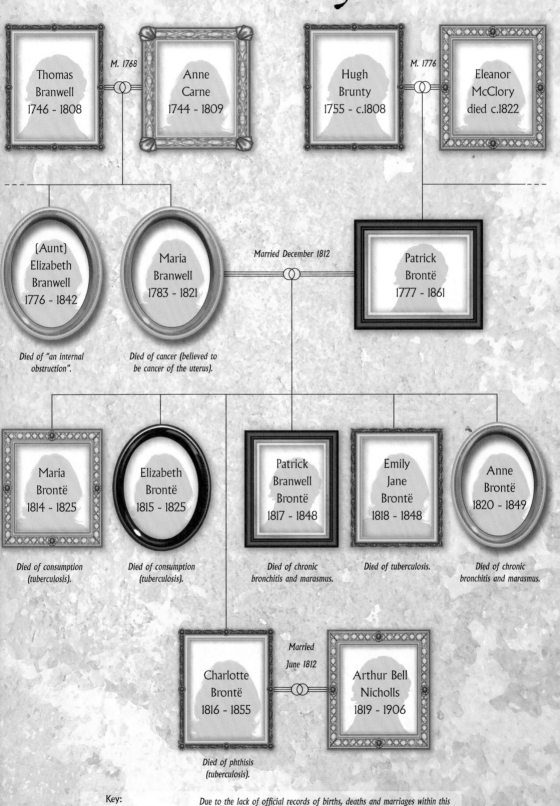

Thomas Branwell 1746 - 1808 — M. 1768 — Anne Carne 1744 - 1809

Hugh Brunty 1755 - c.1808 — M. 1776 — Eleanor McClory died c.1822

(Aunt) Elizabeth Branwell 1776 - 1842

Maria Branwell 1783 - 1821 — Married December 1812 — Patrick Brontë 1777 - 1861

Died of "an internal obstruction".

Died of cancer (believed to be cancer of the uterus).

Maria Brontë 1814 - 1825

Elizabeth Brontë 1815 - 1825

Patrick Branwell Brontë 1817 - 1848

Emily Jane Brontë 1818 - 1848

Anne Brontë 1820 - 1849

Died of consumption (tuberculosis).

Died of consumption (tuberculosis).

Died of chronic bronchitis and marasmus.

Died of tuberculosis.

Died of chronic bronchitis and marasmus.

Charlotte Brontë 1816 - 1855 — Married June 1812 — Arthur Bell Nicholls 1819 - 1906

Died of phthisis (tuberculosis).

Key:
Parent of ———
Married ⚭

Due to the lack of official records of births, deaths and marriages within this period, the above information is derived from extensive research and is as accurate as possible from the limited sources available.

Page Creation

CHAPTER XXXIII

PAGE 142

Panel 1: Nelly at the table pouring tea for Heathcliff, and noticing that YC joyfully sits very near to Hareton, who looks a bit shy of this.

	ORIGINAL TEXT	QUICK TEXT
Nelly Caption	On the morrow, Catherine persuaded Earnshaw to clear a large space of ground from bushes for a flower bed. I was terrified at the devastation; the bushes were the apple of Joseph's eye.	Next day, Catherine asked Hareton to clear some bushes from a part of the garden. The bushes were Joseph's pride and joy.

Panel 2: Heathcliff speaks first to YC, then to Hareton – we enter the conversation half way through here. Its clear that they have been talking about it for a few moments before already. Can this beam done ok within one panel – the thing of him talking to YC first and then switching to looking at Hareton? Its really two 'moments' in time. But we are short of space!

Nelly Caption	Joseph was furious; as was Mr. Heathcliff.	Joseph was furious, and so was Mr. Heathcliff.
Heathcliff	Who the devil gave YOU leave to touch a stick about the place?	Who said you could touch anything in my house?
Heathcliff	And who ordered YOU to obey her?	And who ordered you to do anything for her?

Panel 3: Quick and aggressive backchat between them, show the two of them now, string at each other. She has regained some of her previous defiance, since Hareton is supporting her now.

YC	You shouldn't grudge a few yards of earth for me to ornament, when you have taken all my land!	You should not complain about a small bit of garden when you have taken all of my land!
Heathcliff	Your land, insolent slut? You never had any!	Your land? You never had any!
YC	And my money, and Hareton's land, and his money. Hareton and I are friends now; and I shall tell him all about you!	And my money, and Hareton's land and money.

Panel 4: Heathcliff looks mad and raises himself up.

YC	If you strike me, Hareton will strike you, so you may as well sit down.	Hareton and I are friends now. If you hit me, he will hit you.
Heathcliff	If Hareton does not turn you out of the room, I'll strike him to hell. Damnable witch! dare you pretend to rouse him against me?	If Hareton doesn't throw you out of the room right now, I will strike him to hell! You witch! How dare you turn him against me?

Panel 5: Heathcliff mad, pointing for Nelly to take YC out.

Heathcliff	Off with her! Do you hear? Fling her into the kitchen! I'll kill her, Ellen Dean, if you let her come into my sight again!	Get her out of my sight!

Panel 6: Hareton trying to calm her down, and her looking at him for aid.

Hareton	Wisht! Wisht! I will not hear you speak to him like that. Have done.	You would not speak to him like that.
YC	But you won't let him strike me, would you?	You would not let him hit me, would you?

A page from the script of *Wuthering Heights* showing two versions of the text.

1. Script

In order to create two versions of the same book, the story is first adapted into two scripts: Original Text and Quick Text. While the text differs for each edition, the artwork remains the same for both books.

2. Pencils

Wuthering Heights artist John M. Burns guides us through the process he used to create the artwork:

"Having read and reread the script I produce a thumbnail sketch of the page to decide on how the frames and speech balloons will fit, including a rough layout of the scene to be drawn. The thumbnail is then scaled up to the working page size and transferred to the art board and the frames masked with tape. I then work on the pencil drawings."

A rough thumbnail sketch created from the script.

The pencil drawing of page 142.

3. Inks

"The next process is to ink these drawings. I mix the ink using black, yellow ochre, and burnt umber. This gives the drawings a slight period look and is not such a contrast as black.

When the page is inked in, and I'm happy with everything, I remove the pencil drawing under the ink."

Inked panel with pencil drawing removed.

4. Painting

"Having cleaned the pencil drawing from the inked page, leaving a clean black and white image, I can start the final stage of painting (coloring the page). For this I use a combination of watercolor paint, acrylic ink and acrylic paint."

Starting the coloring process over the inked image.

The finished artwork before lettering.

The finished page 142 with Original Text lettering.

5. Lettering

The final stage is to add the captions, sound effects, and speech bubbles from the script, which are laid on top of each colored page. Two versions of each page are lettered, one for each of the two versions of the book (Original Text and Quick Text).
The lettered pages are then compiled into the two editions of the book.

Original Text

ISBN: 978-1-907127-11-3

Quick Text

ISBN: 978-1-907127-12-0

UR AWARD-WINNING RANGE

Classic Literature in a choice of 2 text versions. Simply choose the text version to match your reading level.

Original Text   THE CLASSIC NOVEL BROUGHT TO LIFE IN FULL COLOR!

Quick Text   THE FULL STORY IN QUICK MODERN ENGLISH FOR A FAST-PACED READ!

Frankenstein: The Graphic Novel   (Mary Shelley)

• Script Adaptation: Jason Cobley • Linework: Declan Shalvey • Art Direction: Jon Haward
• Colors: Jason Cardy & Kat Nicholson • Letters: Terry Wiley

"Cursed be the hands that formed you!"

ISBN: 978-1-906332-49-5

ISBN: 978-1-906332-50-1

• 144 Pages • $16.95

Jane Eyre: The Graphic Novel   (Charlotte Brontë)

• Script Adaptation: Amy Corzine • Artwork: John M. Burns
• Letters: Terry Wiley

"I scorn your idea of love and the counterfeit sentiment you offer. And I scorn you when you offer it."

ISBN: 978-1-906332-47-1

ISBN: 978-1-906332-48-8

• 144 Pages • $16.95

A Christmas Carol: The Graphic Novel   (Charles Dickens)

• Script Adaptation: Seán Michael Wilson • Pencils: Mike Collins
• Inks: David Roach • Colors: James Offredi • Letters: Terry Wiley

"I will honour Christmas in my heart, and try to keep it all the year. I will live in the Past, the Present, and the Future."

ISBN: 978-1-906332-51-8

ISBN: 978-1-906332-52-5

• 160 Pages • $16.95

Great Expectations: The Graphic Novel   (Charles Dickens)

• Script Adaptation: Jen Green • Linework: John Stokes • Coloring: Digikore Studios Ltd
• Color Finishing: Jason Cardy • Letters: Jim Campbell

"I never saw my father or my mother, and never saw any likeness of either of them."

ISBN: 978-1-906332-59-4

ISBN: 978-1-906332-60-0

• 160 Pages • $16.95

To see the complete range, and to view samples online, go to www.classicalcomics.com

DVD-ROM with full audio!

Macbeth
THE INTERACTIVE MOTION COMIC

Macbeth – The Interactive Motion Comic breathes new life into Classical Comics' award-winning Shakespeare play. Unlike no motion comic before, this animated graphic novel boasts a choice of three text versions and a full audio soundtrack.

Sit back and watch Shakespeare's most dramatic tragedy unfold, or take control and switch between Original, Plain and Quick Text versions at the click of a button.

See it, hear it, and fully experience the tragedy that is so feared, no actor will ever say its name...
...Macbeth.

> "Classical Comics is truly inspirational, creating an accessible and fascinating mix of visual and audible drama. The stage and the page brought vividly to life. Highly recommended for any student of Shakespeare!"
>
> *Sir Derek Jacobi,*
> *Actor & Film Director*

Original Text — THE ENTIRE SHAKESPEARE PLAY - UNABRIDGED!

Rollover help notes included

Plain Text — THE ENTIRE PLAY - TRANSLATED INTO PLAIN ENGLISH!

Quick Text — THE ENTIRE PLAY - IN QUICK MODERN ENGLISH!

Click help for an explanation of the features.

Here you can jump to the intro sequence, prologue or the Dramatis Personae

In Original Text mode, hover over highlighted text to view helpful context notes.

You can grab the slider to set the play point of the frame.

Features include:
* All three versions of the animated Classical Comics graphic novel in one application
* Full audio soundtrack
* Helpful context notes accompany the Original Text version
* Links to the Classical Comics graphic novels
* References Act/Scene/Line to link with any traditional script
* Choose 'Movie Mode' to watch the experience unfold or go through the play panel-by-panel
* Runs on any PC (Windows XP SP2 or later), Mac (OS X 10.4.11 or later), or whiteboard

For an online preview visit www.classicalcomics.com/imacbeth